# READY FOR MOORE

## COMING HOME SERIES

ROCHELLE PAIGE

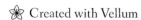

# READY FOR MOORE

From *USA Today* bestselling author Rochelle Paige comes a single-mom, opposites-attract, billionaire romance about coming home and finding love under the worst of circumstances.

Skylar Hicks had nothing in common with the wealthy outsider of the town's founding family. Jumping back into the dating pool with anyone was the last thing she had time for, and certainly not with Baxter Moore after how awful things had gone when they first met.

No matter how gorgeous he was.
Or determined.

After a devastating loss, Baxter's priorities shifted. He left the big city behind so he could reconnect with his extended family. Dating was the last thing on his mind...until Skylar's righteous fury made a big impression. He knew he should stay away from the beautiful single mom, but Baxter couldn't get her out of his mind.

Going after what he wanted had been the key to Baxter's success. And he wanted Skylar. Badly.

He thought coming home would be the biggest change of his life, but he was wrong.

# 1

Even though I'd only spent a few weeks here with my grandparents each summer while I was younger, moving to Mooreville felt like coming home. It royally sucked that it took me almost forty years to realize this was where I'd belonged all along, but I was damn glad to have come to my senses while they were still alive and well.

In their mid-eighties, my grandparents were still a force to be reckoned with. Something they proved yet again with the welcome to Mooreville party they were throwing for me. I'd only moved into my new house six days ago, but here I was, being welcomed back into the bosom of my extended family with open arms.

My grandparents had probably started to

plan this get-together the minute I told them I was thinking about buying some land and building a house on the outskirts of town. Nothing made Franklin and Katherine Moore happier than being surrounded by their family, and they hadn't tried to hide how thrilled they were to have their eldest grandson living only a short drive away. If I'd had any doubts about leaving New York to be closer to them, their reaction would've convinced me that I'd made the right call. My only regret was that I hadn't done it sooner and talked my baby brother into coming with me. Maybe things would've been different if I had.

"I think you missed the memo that this is a party." My cousin Dean sidled up next to me and shoved a red plastic cup into my right hand. He was closest to my age, and we'd spent a lot of time together when I'd visited our grandparents. The bond we'd formed getting into all sorts of trouble together as kids had withstood the test of time and distance. It still paled compared to the relationship he had with the rest of the crew, though.

I glanced down at the icy brown liquid. "What's this?"

"You looked awfully serious for the man of the

hour." He jerked his chin toward the cup. "I figured you could use a drink."

I carefully wiggled the cup side to side. "I know it's a drink, but what kind?"

"Rum and Coke." He chuckled and shrugged. "What else would it be?"

Rum and Coke was my grandfather's signature drink—and the first alcoholic beverage I'd ever tried —but I couldn't remember the last time I'd had rum in anything. Probably when I was in town for Christmas two years ago. I was more of a single malt whisky kind of guy. But he was right—I should've known what was in the cup before I asked since Dean took after our grandfather in a lot of ways.

"Good point." I took a sip and tried my best to hide my grimace. The combination was too sweet for my taste, no matter how good the rum was. "Rigden supplied the alcohol?"

"Always," Dean confirmed with a grin. "Having a cousin who owns an artisan distillery definitely doesn't suck."

Since I'd provided the start-up funds, Rigden kept me in the loop about what he was working on. Including shipping me samples of every new batch of spirits. "Did he bring any of that rye whiskey he started making at the end of last year?"

"Probably." He jerked his chin toward where a makeshift bar had been set up on my grandmother's sideboard in the dining room. "The first thing I saw was the rum, so I didn't look any further. But a ton of bottles are back there. Seemed to me that he brought pretty much everything."

Rigden's rye was spicier than my favorite whisky, but some of it on the rocks was more to my taste than a rum and Coke. Noticing that his cup was almost empty, I handed Dean back the one he'd given me. "Here, take this. I'll get myself something else soon."

"Your loss." He dumped the remainder of his drink into the cup and slipped the full cup into the empty one. "How's the estate treating you? Did you get moved in okay?"

I sighed and shook my head. "You sold me the damn thing, you should know better than anyone that it's just a house, Dean."

"Yeah, and my commission on that house"—he made air quotes with his fingers—"was more than I made all of last year."

"You more than earned it," I echoed what I'd told my cousin when he'd tried to talk me into cutting the percentage on his commission. With what I'd paid for the acreage plus the construction costs, the deal hadn't been insignificant. But Dean had been my eyes and ears on the sale, finding me the perfect lot and acting as the project manager for the build since I was halfway across the country for most of the process.

"In hindsight, I have to admit that you're right." He took a swig of his drink and grinned at me. "The place did turn out pretty damn awesome."

I didn't have any complaints. By the time I'd gotten into town, all I'd needed to do was collect the keys from Dean. The interior designer had already decorated the entire place, and the staff who'd chosen to make the move with me had arrived a week earlier. Other than writing the checks, there had been very little for me to do. "I couldn't have done it without you."

"Damn straight." He flashed me a cocky grin. "I should've asked for a bonus. That's how good of a job I did."

I jerked my chin toward the stacked red plastic cups he was holding. "Feel free to consider that your bonus."

He cocked his head to the side. "The drink I brought you?"

"Yeah."

"Is that the secret to becoming a billionaire? Being a cheapskate who is shameless enough to regift something back to the original giver?" He chuckled over the rim of the cup before taking another sip.

"Considering rum and Coke is your drink of choice and not mine, you probably brought the damn thing over here knowing I'd hand it right back to you." I'd been joking around, but judging by the gleam in his eyes, I was actually right.

"Could be." He wagged his brows. "But you'll never know for sure."

I punched him in the shoulder just hard enough for him to really feel it. "Asshole."

"Guilty as charged." He finished the rest of the drink. "Just don't let my mom hear you call me that. You know I'm her favorite."

"Not even close," Wyatt muttered as he joined us. "I'm the youngest. That automatically makes me the favorite."

"No, it just means you're the baby," Dean disagreed with a glare at his little brother who wasn't so little anymore.

"That's because although you should be old enough to take care of yourself by now, you're the only one of us who technically still lives at home."

"Only during the summer when school is out," Wyatt grumbled. He was twenty-six and had just started his final year of his Doctor of Pharmacy program at Purdue, so I understood his irritation. Dean made it sound as though he was a slacker who still lived in his parents' basement.

"Rationalize it however you want, bro"—Wyatt flashed him a smug grin—"but we both know it's just your jealousy talking because Mom makes my favorites for dinner even when you come over."

The narrowing of Dean's eyes let us both know that his brother's verbal barb had landed true. "What're you even doing here? Don't you have classes to attend or a paper to write?"

"I drove in for the weekend so I could come to the party." Wyatt lifted his cup toward me. "Cheers, welcome, and all that shit."

"Thanks."

His gaze dropped to my empty hands. "Damn, sorry, I should've brought a drink over for you."

"No worries," I assured him. "I was just about to head over to grab one."

"You gonna bring me back another?" Dean asked.

"Sure." I shot him a sly glance. "But don't be surprised if it's a whiskey on the rocks."

He laughed, and I walked away as his brother asked him what was so funny. It took me a while to make my way over to the bar since I was stopped by my other cousins, aunts, and uncles along the way. And there were a ton of them.

My dad's side of the family was prolific. My dad was the only one who didn't fit the pattern since he and my mom only had Weston and me. He was the eldest of four boys, and each of his brothers had three sons of their own. Dean, Wyatt, and Jude belonged to Uncle Mike and Aunt Beth. Uncle Bruce and Aunt Patty had Rigden, Finn, and Logan. And my dad's youngest brother, Chuck, and his wife, Sally, rounded out the group with Ryland, Silas, and Ethan. The Moore clan had a whole lot of testosterone and no estrogen, with the exception of the women who married into the family.

Our generation hadn't carried on the legacy yet— a fact my mother lamented over all the time. She'd been ready for grandchildren more than a decade ago and wasn't happy that I'd hit forty without getting married and having babies. I'd been focused on building an empire and tuned her complaints out for years. It had only been in the past year that I had started to wonder if she might have a point. I had more than enough money to last me several lifetimes, and I wasn't getting any younger.

My grandfather glanced up from the drink he'd been pouring, a concerned gleam filling his eyes as he scanned my face. "You look like you have the weight of the world on your shoulders. We should've given you more time to settle into your new home before we threw you a party."

"Don't worry about me, Grandpa. Most of my things were already unpacked before I arrived in town, and I've had more than enough time to get accustomed to the house." I flashed him a quick grin as I reached for a cup and the bottle of rye whiskey. "This party was the perfect excuse to force me to socialize before I turned into a hermit."

"Good." He clapped me on the back. "Then maybe you're ready for your first official event as a citizen of Mooreville."

I glanced around the room, my brows drawing together. "This isn't it?"

"Not even close." He shook his head with a chuckle. "This is just a family get-together."

He had me there. The party was huge, but everyone in attendance was related to me in one way or another. "What's the difference when our family makes up half the population of the town?"

"Unlike when my great-great-great-grandfather settled here, our family is vastly outnumbered now. Mooreville has grown quite a bit since you were little." The approval in his eyes was impossible to miss, which only made me feel guiltier over what he said next. "In large part because of you, even though your visits were so rare."

Before I turned eighteen, I visited them every summer without fail. But after I got an internship with my dad's company between my freshman and sophomore years, I started putting off my trips to Indiana for when I didn't have quite so much going on. Only something more important always seemed to come up, and my visits became fewer with larger gaps between them. "I'm sorry I didn't spend more time with you guys after I started college. I don't have much of an excuse, except that I was young and dumb."

"Your grandmother and I understood how busy you were." The hint of sadness in his eyes made me wonder if he was thinking about my dad, who hadn't stepped foot in Mooreville in more years than I could remember. He couldn't wait to get out of Mooreville when he was younger and had never looked back after he left for college. "We were just happy that you took such a liking to this place that you kept coming back after you were all grown up, even though it wasn't as often as we might have liked."

"Well, you're stuck with me now because I'm not going anywhere."

"We can't change the past. Now is all that counts." He squeezed my forearm. "And you're in good company. We have so many new residents because of how much our downtown has boomed over the past decade or so. Thanks to you."

"You're the one who deserves the credit. I would never have thought to invest in Mooreville real estate without the push you gave me." He seemed uncomfortable with my praise, so I shifted the conversation back to my civic duties. "What's the event you were talking about?"

My grandfather took a sip of his drink before explaining, "The county is going to be auctioning off some vehicles tomorrow at the impound lot."

I wasn't sure why he thought I'd be interested in the auction. "I'm not in the market for a car. I just bought a new truck, and the transportation company is going to deliver my Tesla and Bentley."

"I'll never understand how one man needs three cars." He sighed and shook his head.

"Then why are you trying to talk me into getting a fourth?" I asked, twisting the cap back onto the bottle of rye after pouring myself a few fingers over a couple of ice cubes.

"I figured you'd be interested since the money

from the auction is going to be used for the widows and orphans fund."

My difficulty swallowing the whiskey I'd just taken a sip of had nothing to do with the burn of the liquor as it went down my throat. I hadn't been prepared for his explanation. "Thanks for the heads-up. I'll be there."

"Whatever you do, don't bid on lot number twenty," he warned. "Crushing the dreams of a local boy would be a bad introduction to the people you aren't related to in Mooreville."

I'd never been to an auction before, let alone one run by the county to sell off vehicles they didn't want to keep in their fleet any longer. But ever since my son had heard about them and told me what he wanted to do, I'd learned as much as I could about the process. Even armed with all the information I'd found online, I was still nervous as we crossed the county's impound lot. Simon would be devastated if things didn't go his way today, and I couldn't do anything else to guarantee he'd walk away with the vehicle he so desperately wanted to buy.

"Good afternoon, Skylar." Mark, Mooreville's fire chief for the past decade, smiled at me before he shifted his attention to my teenage son. "Did you remember to bring all that money you've been saving up?"

Simon shook his head and laughed. "Nah, but I did bring my debit card. My checkbook too, in case they can't take a card."

Mark quirked a brow. "Have you ever even written a check before?"

"Nope, this would be my first." The hint of sadness that flashed in his eyes for a moment broke my heart. "I guess that kinda makes it more special in a way."

"It sure does." Mark clasped my son's shoulder and gave him a quick squeeze. "Your dad would've been so proud of how hard you worked to make this happen today."

"I'm not in the clear yet, sir." Simon looked around the crowded lot, his Adam's apple bobbing in his throat. "A lot of people are here. Someone could outbid me."

I flung my arm around his back, remembering a time when I could easily have reached his shoulders instead. I could barely wrap my head around the fact that he was going to have his driver's license soon. Time was flying by, and he was growing so quickly. "Everyone in town knows what today means to you."

His dad had been the county fire marshal, and

the marked vehicle he'd used while on duty was up for auction today. As soon as Simon knew there was a chance for him to own his dad's SUV, he'd stopped spending money on video games and other junk he'd previously been convinced was necessary. Every penny he had earned shoveling snow and mowing yards for our neighbors for the past two years had been set aside for today. Same with the cash his grandparents had given him for his birthday and holidays.

Somehow, he had managed to save up a little more than three thousand bucks. I'd offered to match him dollar for dollar, so I felt pretty good about his chances at being the winning bid, even if he went up against an out-of-towner who didn't know why nobody else was interested in that particular lot.

Word had quickly spread around Mooreville when Simon started saving up—secrets tended to be difficult to keep in small towns. Plenty of people had hired him when they didn't truly need the help. And their support hadn't ended there. I'd been stopped by pretty much all of our neighbors so they could assure me that everyone had been warned off Steven's SUV after the auction's date was announced.

Mark pointed toward a school bus on our left where they'd set up a makeshift office out the back.

"You'll want to head over there to check in. After your mom signs some paperwork, they'll give her a bidder card and the auction list. Your dad's SUV is the last lot, number twenty."

Simon's nose wrinkled, and I knew it was because he wasn't happy to get confirmation that I was the one who'd be doing the bidding today. "C'mon, kiddo. You heard the chief."

"This blows. I should be able to do this on my own since it's my money," Simon grumbled as we walked over to the school bus. We'd already had this discussion this morning over breakfast, when he noticed that his checks required my signature too since it was a joint account with spending limits set in place for Simon because he was a minor.

There was only one person ahead of us when we reached the back of the line. I turned my back toward them and lowered my voice as I said, "Like I already told you, the car will be yours as far as I'm concerned. I'm not going to hold it over your head or take it away from you as a punishment like I have to do sometimes with your video game console."

"Unless I do something super stupid like drink and drive"—he paused to roll his eyes and heave a deep sigh—"which will never happen because I know better."

Even with his tone and teenage attitude, I beamed him an approving smile. "And as soon as you're old enough, we'll transfer over the paperwork."

"Which is gonna be like...forever." He kicked the gravel beneath his feet.

Reaching up, I ruffled his hair, earning me a death glare. Ever since Simon had started his sophomore year and became interested in girls, he'd gotten picky about every aspect of his looks. His usual athletic shorts and T-shirts with funny sayings were replaced by button-downs and polos with khakis. He went from me needing to pester him to take a shower to using up all the hot water each morning. He also wanted to go for a haircut every six weeks, asked for all kinds of hair product—some that I had no idea existed—and switched his shampoo and conditioner. Touching the hair was definitely a no-go.

"Next," the person handling auction registrations called.

After I filled out the required paperwork and got my bidding number, Simon and I circled the gravel lot until we stood in front of Steven's old work vehicle. I hadn't ridden in the red SUV often since we normally used my car when he wasn't on shift for the fire department, but that didn't stop me from feeling nostalgic as I stared through the windshield. I'd been so focused on helping my son get what he wanted that I hadn't stopped to think about how I'd feel having a reminder of my past sitting in my driveway every day.

But my pain didn't matter—only Simon's happiness. That was the mantra I'd lived by for the past five years, and I wasn't about to change it now. So I pasted a smile on my face and bumped his arm with my shoulder. "Are you ready to own your first car?"

Unlike mine, his grin was genuine. "Beyond ready."

"And pretty soon, you'll even be able to drive it all by yourself." The timing of the auction was almost perfect. Simon had gotten his learner's permit four months ago and only had two more to go before he could get his license.

"Finally," he grumbled with another kick at the gravel.

"C'mon, let's head over to where they're going to do the bidding before you wear a hole in the bottom of your shoe."

Since he was wearing his favorite pair of sneakers for good luck, I didn't get any pushback as we walked over to the folding chairs they had set up near the school bus check-in area. I was fidgety while we waited, my knee bouncing and my fingers tapping against my thigh.

After about ten minutes, Simon reached over and pressed his hand on top of mine, flattening my palm against my leg. "You're gonna do great, Mom."

I had such a great kid. He had every reason to be more nervous than I was, but he still wanted to give me a pep talk. "Let's hope so because I don't have any more time to prepare. It looks as though they're ready to begin."

Simon's head jerked forward, and his focus stayed on the auctioneer as he took bids for all of the other vehicles they were selling today. It wasn't until they finally got to Steven's SUV that he turned to me again. "I feel like I'm gonna barf."

"Aim it that way if you do." I pointed toward the other side of his body and sent up a quick mental thanks that we were on the end of our row of chairs.

He laughed and shook his head. "Gee, thanks for all the motherly concern."

"Sorry, but I'm already in mom mode for the auction." I jerked my chin toward the auctioneer as I gripped my bidder card. "All of my focus needs to be on these bids, just in case we're up against anyone else."

"Good point." His Adam's apple bobbed in his

throat as the minimum bid was announced. The words were barely out of the auctioneer's mouth before my hand went up in the air.

"Two thousand dollars." Unlike with the other lots, the auctioneer didn't give anyone else time to counterbid before he started to call, "Going once, going twice, and—"

A split second before he had the chance to say "sold," a deep voice shouted, "Fifty thousand dollars."

The silence following that outrageous bid was so complete, you could've heard a pin drop. Even the birds stopped chirping. Or maybe I just couldn't hear them over the thundering of my heart in my ears.

But I didn't miss the auctioneer's stuttered, "S-s-sold."

I couldn't remember ever being quite so furious with someone before. That SUV hadn't even cost fifty thousand dollars when the county had bought it for Steven to use seven years ago after he'd been promoted to fire marshal. I couldn't think of one decent reason somebody would be willing to pay that much for a vehicle that was worth the fraction of the cost.

His decision made no sense...and it had destroyed my son. The joy I'd seen on Simon's face only seconds ago had been replaced by anguish. He'd been so close to the dream he'd worked so hard to accomplish until that man had stolen it out from under him. He sat next to me, not moving a muscle as a lone tear streaked down his cheek.

Leaning into his side, I placed my hand over his and squeezed. "Breathe, Simon."

His chest expanded and caved back in as he gulped for air, his shoulders shaking with the effort it took to hold himself together.

"I'm so freaking sorry, sweetie."

He shook his head, too overcome with emotion to say anything. The same wasn't true for me. They'd saved Steven's vehicle for last, so I didn't have to wait long to confront the man who had caused my son so much pain. I fumed during the fifteen minutes it took him to complete his transaction. A few strokes of his pen, made while Simon stared down at the auction booklet, and the deed was done. My son hadn't moved an inch since the auctioneer had pounded his gavel against the podium that last time.

Before I jumped out of my chair, I murmured, "Stay put. I'll be right back."

Simon was lost in his head and didn't react to my words. I cast him one last worried look before I stormed over to the man who'd earned himself a piece of my mind. Even in my fury, I didn't miss how gorgeous he was. With his chiseled jawline, piercing gray eyes, and tall, muscular frame, he was unapologetically masculine. Even the man bun he'd pulled his brown hair into didn't take away from his manliness. And the hint of gray in his beard and mustache only added to it.

"Do you have any idea what you've done?" I hissed, not even bothering to try to keep my voice down. Most of the people surrounding us knew why Simon and I were here. None of them would be surprised by my reaction to the stunt this guy had just pulled. My gaze raked down his tall body, taking in the cut of the suit jacket he'd paired with his designer jeans and Italian leather shoes. "You must have more money than brain cells because you just paid more than ten times what that vehicle is worth."

His lips curved into a small smirk that I longed to smack from his face. "Not quite. That'd put me in the top ten of the world's wealthiest billionaires when I barely squeaked my way onto the list last year."

I flung my hand in the air, my palm facing him. "Do. Not. Even."

He pretended to zip his lips together, and I felt as though my head was about to explode. I didn't think I'd ever been this angry before, and the man had the gall to look like he was about to laugh at me.

Planting my hands on my hips—so I didn't haul off and punch him—I leaned closer. "My son has been dreaming about owning that SUV you just bought on a whim for years. While you're standing there feeling proud because you're the big man in town who just dropped big money that'll help the widows and orphans in the county, you crushed the dreams of one of them beneath the soles of your shoes...that probably also cost way more than you needed to spend."

The humor drained from his expression, and his lips parted. Before he could say something else to set me off, I shook my head. "Just don't. I don't want to hear anything you have to say since you can't go back in time and undo what you've already done. But hey, thanks for teaching my son a lesson about how unfair life is, as if he didn't already know that way better than any child should."

I turned on my heel, glancing over my shoulder for one final verbal jab. "I hope the damn SUV breaks down every single time you drive it."

I didn't understand the flare of approval in his gray eyes, not until he stalked past me to where my son was still sitting and dropped the title and keys onto his lap. When Simon's head jerked up, the man murmured, "I didn't mean to upset you. I just wanted to make a donation to the fund. Figured you could use all that money you earned for upkeep and insurance instead."

He didn't give Simon or me time to react before he strode over to a brand-new Rivian truck and climbed in the driver's side. There was some murmuring around us, but I didn't pay attention to what anyone was saying because my entire focus was on my son. His eyes were wide as he stared down at the keys in his hand. "Did that really happen?"

"Yeah, kiddo. It really did." I wasn't quite sure exactly how or why, and my brain was still trying to catch up, but there was no mistaking what the hot guy I'd just publicly reamed out had done for my son.

"Dad's truck is mine now? And I get to keep the money?"

"Looks like it."

Simon turned to stare at the man's truck as it pulled out of the lot. "Who was that guy?"

I didn't know, but I would have to find out. I owed him one heck of an apology.

## 3

BAXTER

Every second of the blonde's diatribe played in my head over and over again during the drive home. She was magnificent in her fury, with her blue eyes spitting fire, her chest heaving, and her cheeks tinged pink. My body hadn't given a damn that she was ripping me a new one in front of an audience who didn't try to hide their curiosity. Or that the story was certain to get back to my grandparents before the end of the day. Probably in the next hour.

Calling my grandpa to give him a heads-up would've been smart, but no way could I talk to him while my dick was rock-hard. I was beyond ready for that woman to work out her anger in another way. In bed. Naked. With me. Slamming her pussy up and down my shaft in a brutal, punishing pace.

I could picture us having sex too damn easily, and it wasn't helping my hard-on go down. I left her gaping at me thirty minutes ago, and I still had to adjust myself before I climbed out of my truck after parking in front of my house. At forty years old, I had long since passed the time when I spontaneously sported a woody over a woman I hadn't even touched. But I hadn't seen anything like her before—a mother ready to go to battle for her son. She was so damn gorgeous, and I wanted that fire in my life.

"What in the hell were you thinking, Baxter?"

I whirled around at the sound of my cousin's voice. He'd been at the auction, too. I must have been too wrapped up in my fantasies to notice that he'd followed me home.

Dean slammed his car door. "I get that we haven't had the chance to hang out much in the past twenty or so years, but I thought you were smarter than that."

"Not sure what you're talking about," I murmured, leaning a hip against my truck.

He scrubbed his palms down his face. "C'mon. You have to know that you could've handled the whole thing a fuck of a lot better than you did."

"Handled what better?" I growled, pissed that he thought I was the one in the wrong in this situation.

It wasn't as though he'd heard about the whole thing secondhand. He'd been there to see what went down and knew as well as anyone that my motives were pure. "Donating fifty grand to the widows and orphans fund? Or giving that kid a free car?"

"Both."

My head reared back at his answer. "You're kidding me, right?"

Dean held his hands up in a gesture of surrender. "I'm not saying you did a bad thing back there, but you just as easily could have given a check to the fire chief without coming to the auction."

I didn't bother to mention that I'd done just that last year when the local department had needed some new equipment and the chief had reached out to me through my grandfather. "And the kid?"

"You should have talked to his mom first. Maybe then she wouldn't have been pissed as fuck at you." He shook his head and sighed. "Although, knowing Skylar, she never would have gone for your plan anyway. So maybe it is better that you didn't talk to her first because she got your help whether she wanted it or not."

*Skylar.* She had a beautiful name to go with that gorgeous face. "You really think she would have turned me down?"

"Hell yeah, I do." My cousin knew me well enough to recognize how surprised I was by how certain he sounded. "That woman is as stubborn as they come."

"Stubborn?" I echoed, my dick inexplicably straining against my zipper at the description.

"Skylar is nothing like the pampered debutantes that your parents keep throwing at you," Dean warned. "She's raised that boy on her own for the past five years, with a little bit of help from her in-laws. And that's only because she didn't want her son to lose his relationship with his closest set of grandparents since her parents live in Florida."

He sounded as though he knew Skylar well, which made sense, considering how small Mooreville was. But I wasn't happy about it when I didn't know anything about her other than her name—which he'd given me—and that she had a teenage son. "Is she a close friend of yours?"

"What?" His brows drew together as he shook his head. "No, I've only talked to her a few times, but her situation was a hot topic back when her husband died."

I lowered my head to stare at the ground and mumbled, "Shit, I figured there was a story behind the kid wanting that SUV so badly."

"It was his dad's." Dean's eyes were filled with worry as he scanned my expression. "He wasn't killed in the line of duty, though. He started out as a firefighter but worked his way up to fire marshal. It was a boating accident. He was out fishing in the middle of the lake and collided with another boat. Hit his head before he went in the water and didn't come back up."

I hadn't realized I was holding my breath until I exhaled deeply, my shoulders slumping. "I'm glad I could help him get the vehicle and do some good at the same time."

"Look, I get why the fire department is near and dear to your heart." I fisted my hands, my knuckles turning white, and Dean's gaze dropped down to them. "I wasn't as close to him as you were, but I miss Weston, too."

Hearing my baby brother's name felt like a punch in the gut. It had been almost a full year, but I felt his loss as keenly as I had the day I'd gotten the news. "Then you've gotta understand why I did what I did at the auction."

"Here's the thing, though." Dean moved closer, coming to a stop about a foot in front of me. "I don't think your reasons for bidding on that car were as altruistic as you're making them out to be."

Considering I'd had no intention of buying anything at the auction when I went there, it was a fair assumption. But that didn't mean I was going to confess my reasons to him so easily. "Why else would I have done it other than to make sure the widows and orphans fund has all the money they need?"

"Because you wanted to impress Skylar."

"I'm not the kind of guy who tosses money around to gain a woman's attention." Or at least I never had been until today. "And definitely not ones I don't even know."

"Yeah, and that's what makes this whole situation even stranger." Dean crossed his arms over his chest. "I know Grandpa warned you not to bid on that lot. I asked him about it when he mentioned that he talked to you about the auction. Everyone in town knew about Simon's plan to buy his dad's vehicle, but you haven't been here long. I was worried you'd be the only one out of the loop, and you'd mess the whole thing up for the kid."

"You should've had more faith in me, cuz. I didn't mess anything up for the kid." I winced a little as I thought about how crushed he'd looked before I'd explained that the SUV was his, free and clear. "He was better off for me being there and bidding on the vehicle he wanted and so is the widows and orphans fund."

"Here's the thing, though." He paused to make sure he had my full attention. "You need to leave her alone."

I couldn't believe what I was hearing. "Are you warning me off a woman?"

"Yeah, I am."

"Why? Are you calling dibs? We haven't done stupid shit like that since we were teenagers, man." The thought of my cousin with the beautiful single mom had my fists clenching tighter.

Dean shook his head. "No, I'm not one of the guys in town who have tried to talk Skylar into a date."

With her looks and personality, I wasn't surprised to hear that Skylar had lots of men sniffing around her. "Tried?"

"From what I've heard, she must've loved her husband very much." If my hard-on hadn't already gone down, that information would've done it. "He's been dead for five years, and she hasn't gone out with another guy even once. No coffee dates, no lunches, and sure as fuck no dinner and dancing. And it's not because she's been lacking offers, although they mostly come from out-of-towners nowadays because the men in Mooreville know better than to ask her out."

At least I didn't have to worry about a local man interfering with my plans for Skylar. Which was a lucky thing since it sounded like it was going to take me some time to convince the grieving widow to give me a chance. "Is that so?"

"Fucking hell," he groaned, running a hand through his hair. "I'm not going to be able to talk you out of pursuing her, am I?"

I shook my head. "Nope."

Dean's eyes narrowed. "You saw her for what, an hour? Tops?"

I spotted Skylar making her way around the gravel lot as soon as I arrived. Her back had been toward me, and my gaze had been glued to her fantastic ass until she turned around, and I was stunned to see that the view was even better from the front. "Yup."

"During which time she reamed you a new one?"

My lips curved into a smirk. "Uh-huh."

"And you're actually smiling about it." He let out a low whistle. "I hate to be the one to break it to you, but something is seriously wrong with you."

My smile widened. "You're probably right."

"But that's not going to stop you from going after her."

It was a statement instead of a question, but I answered anyway. "Nope, not a chance in hell."

He tapped his index finger against his chin. "Then I guess there's only one thing I can do."

I quirked a brow. "What's that?"

"I'm going to have to help you get the girl." He grinned as he pretended to salute me. "Dean Moore, reporting for wingman duty."

**4**

"Mmm, is that chocolate sheet cake I smell?"

I flashed Simon a quick smile over my shoulder. "It sure is."

"Yum." He patted his belly. "My favorite."

I bent low to pull the second jelly roll pan out of the oven. "Which is why I made two."

"Two?" He gasped, rounding the kitchen counter to stare at the cakes. "Did I forget it's my birthday or something?"

I laughed and shook my head as I yanked the oven mitts off my hands. "There's no chance of that happening, especially this year when you're counting down the days more than usual."

"Only eighty-nine to go until I get my license." He dipped his index finger into the saucepan on the stovetop, then lifted it to suck a dab of frosting from the tip.

When he reached out for more, I gently slapped his hand to stop him. "No double dipping. Germs."

"But you don't like frosting. You're not even going to put it on your part," he complained.

"Only one of the cakes is for us." I nudged him out of the way with my hip so I could stir the mixture of melted butter, milk, and cocoa. It was almost ready for me to add the vanilla and confectioner's sugar before pouring over the warm cakes.

A wrinkle popped up in the middle of his forehead. "Who's the other one for?"

"Baxter Moore."

It hadn't taken much effort to find out the name of the man who had given Steven's SUV to Simon at the auction yesterday. Although he only moved to town a week ago, everyone seemed to know who he was—except for me.

Mark had approached us after everything went down to make sure we were okay. Simon smiled and told him that he was awesome, while my cheeks filled with heat over how I'd lit into the man who'd handed my son his dream, only better. The fire chief told me not to be embarrassed since I'd only been protecting my son like any good parent would do.

Then he'd blown my mind when he explained who Baxter was.

I hadn't needed more than his name to understand why he wanted to make a big donation to the widows and orphans' fund. I had already heard about what happened to his younger brother a year ago. Anything having to do with the Moores was big news around here, even the branch of the family who didn't call Mooreville home.

"Good call on the apology dessert. Nobody can resist your chocolate sheet cake."

"Let's hope you're right," I muttered, finishing the frosting and pouring it over about two-thirds of the first cake and all of the second. Baking him a cake seemed like a great idea an hour ago, but now I was second-guessing myself. My chocolate sheet cake was the first to go at every potluck, but Baxter wasn't like the rest of his family. He was a freaking billionaire. The closest he probably came to eating chocolate cake was a fancy soufflé made by a famous French chef.

"Are you taking it to him today while I'm at school?" Simon asked.

"Yup, that's the plan." As long as I didn't chicken out.

Simon glanced at the clock on the stove. "Great, I

have just enough time to write him a quick note before the bus comes."

"A note?" I echoed, my eyes widening as I stared at my son's back while he darted out of the kitchen.

His voice drifted toward me as he yelled, "Yeah, I think I owe him a thank-you, don't you?"

I absolutely did. What I hadn't expected was for my teenager to come up with the idea on his own. Not when I could barely get him to sign a thank-you card for his grandparents after his birthday each year. Then again, they'd never gotten him a car, let alone the one his dad had used as a fire marshal.

An hour later, armed with a cake and Simon's note—which he hadn't let me read—I inched my way down the long driveway that led to Baxter Moore's new home. The gate had been open when I pulled up, and the truck he'd been in yesterday was parked in front of the mansion I'd heard so much about over the past six months. The place was even bigger than I expected, a sprawling two-story brick house with impeccable landscaping and a huge front porch.

I was so jittery as I walked toward the front door, the pan shook from how much my hands were trembling. Afraid that I'd drop the cake when I rang the doorbell, I used my shoulder to lean against the button. While the bell chimed, I took a few deep breaths to help calm my nerves. Not that it did me much good since my hands grew damp as the door opened.

The man who greeted me wasn't the one I'd been expecting, but maybe that was for the best, considering the magnetic pull I'd felt toward Baxter Moore yesterday. He was cute—with short blond hair and blue eyes—and appeared to be about my age, but there wasn't any spark between us. Handing the cake over to him was a much safer option, and I'd learned the hard way not to take unnecessary risks with my heart.

"Hello," he greeted with a smile. "How may I help you?"

"Could you give this to Mr. Moore for me please?" I asked, extending my arms to shove the cake toward him.

He instinctively reached out to grab the pan when it was inches from his stomach. "I'd be more than happy to do so, but wouldn't you rather give it to him yourself? My boss is quite partial to sweets, and chocolate is his favorite. I'm certain he'll want to thank you for the lovely cake himself."

"There's really no need." I tapped the note that I had taped to the lid of the pan, grateful that Simon had given me the perfect out. "This explains everything."

"What needs an explanation?" a deep, masculine —and unfortunately, familiar—voice asked.

I pressed my lips together to stop myself from sighing when Baxter appeared behind his employee, looking every bit as sexy as he had yesterday. His gray sports coat strained against his broad shoulders, the top two buttons of his white dress shirt were unbuttoned, and his hair was pulled back again. Although his outfit probably cost more than every-thing in my closet combined, there was still a rough edge to his look that really did it for me.

I took a step back as I lifted my hand in an awkward wave. "Hey."

Baxter's gaze swept down the length of my body, and I was happy that I'd had the foresight to put some extra effort into my appearance this morning. My blond hair was pulled back in a braid, I'd done my eye makeup a little heavier than usual, and I'd gone with a pair of jeans I hadn't worn in years. They fit me like a glove and made my butt look great.

I really should've reconsidered this plan when I'd dug them out from the bottom of a dresser drawer. I hadn't given much thought to what I looked like in years, and less than twenty-four hours after meeting this man, I suddenly cared way more than I should.

"I've got this, Paul," Baxter murmured as he took the cake pan.

"Sure thing, boss." Paul flashed me a quick smile before walking away, leaving me alone with Baxter.

When he was out of earshot, Baxter gestured for me to come inside his home.

"Oh, no. That's okay," I muttered, taking another step back as I shook my head. "I just wanted to stop by and drop that off."

His lips curved into a grin as he glanced down at the pan. "You baked me a cake?"

I shrugged, my cheeks filling with heat. "I figured it's the least I could do after how I yelled at you at the auction yesterday. I am so sorry for going off on you like that."

"The last thing you need to do is apologize to me." He stepped out onto the porch, balancing the cake pan in one hand as he used the other to shut the door behind him, giving us more privacy. "My heart was in the right place, but I handled the situation all wrong. If I'd given you a heads-up about what I planned, your son wouldn't have gotten so upset and there wouldn't have been any need for you to protect him."

"Wow. Okay," I breathed, surprised by how easily he admitted to his part in what went down between us.

His grin widened. "You were expecting me to be pissed, huh?"

"Uh, yeah." I swept my arm toward his home. "Aren't rich East Coasters supposed to be rude and unfriendly?"

"I've met more than my fair share of gruff New Yorkers." He chuckled and shook his head. "But my grandparents did their best to instill their Midwest values in me every time I visited when I was young."

"They sure did succeed." I shoved my hands into my pockets and rocked back on my heels. "What you did for Simon yesterday was more than generous."

He shrugged. "Like I told him, I was already going to make the donation anyway. It was just a case of being in the right place at the right time to be able to help him out a little."

"It was a pretty big deal to Simon." I inched forward the tiniest bit, intrigued by how he was downplaying what he'd done when most people would be bragging.

"Which was why I didn't just write a check without bidding on anything." He closed the remaining space between us, the cake pan acting as a buffer between our bodies. "My grandfather told me how hard your boy worked to raise that money. You should be proud of what he accomplished."

"I am." My deep breath to calm my nerves back-fired because I ended up dragging his scent into my nostrils. Holy heck, he smelled good. "Which only makes me more grateful for what you did yesterday. Now he gets the best of both worlds—knowing he could've bought the car by himself but getting to keep the money he earned, so he doesn't have to worry if something goes wrong with it. Buying his dad's work vehicle was his dream, and your generosity means he'll be able to keep it longer than I expected. Thank you."

"You're welcome." A hint of sadness filled his gray eyes, and I clenched my hand to keep myself from reaching out to comfort him in whatever small way I could. "I'm glad I could help give your son something that means so much to him. Losing someone you love is difficult."

Thanks to how quickly gossip spread in Moore-ville, I knew he was talking about his brother's death almost a year ago. Although his branch of the family barely spent any time in town, it had still been big news. "Simon has had five years to adapt to life without his dad, but your loss is still new. I'm so sorry. You have my deepest sympathies."

"Thank you." He heaved a deep sigh and shook his head. "That's one of the things I'll have to get used to with the move. There isn't any anonymity around here. Not that I got a ton of it in New York either, since I found myself on gossip pages more often than I'd have liked."

"I'm sure you were." Considering he was a hot, single billionaire, I wasn't surprised. "But it's kind of weird knowing something so personal about you when I don't really know you at all."

"Seems fair to me since I've already heard about how you lost your husband in a boating accident. I'm sorry for Simon's and your loss as well."

My back straightened at the reminder of Steven. "Thanks. Small towns, huh?"

His lips curved into a half-smile. "I'm quickly learning it's impossible to keep a secret around here."

"Nearly," I mumbled under my breath as I took a step back.

"There's a surefire way for us to get past the awkwardness of knowing stuff about each other when we're basically strangers."

My body tightened up as my eyes widened. "Pardon?"

"By getting to know each other." His half-smile turned into a sexy smirk that had butterflies swirling in my belly. "Let me take you out to dinner."

I'd been asked out plenty of times since Steven died, but I'd never been tempted to accept. Until now.

Baxter Moore was a dangerous man, at least to the wall I'd built to protect myself. "Sorry, but it's going to have to be a no for dinner."

Although Dean had warned me about Skylar's resistance to dating, her rejection had stung. Had it not been for the regret that had shone from her pretty blue eyes that let me know she was tempted, I might've spent the next few days wallowing over the encounter. Then again, I'd never been one to easily admit defeat. I sure as hell wasn't going to start now.

But I was still a little grumpy when my cousin called Wednesday morning. Skipping the usual greeting, I growled, "What in the world could you possibly need this early in the morning? I'm basically retired, remember?"

His laughter drifted through the line. "I hate to break it to you, but with the size of your real estate portfolio, you'll never truly be retired. Also, nine thirty isn't that early, even for retirees."

"That's fair, but my limited to-do list means I can start my mornings as late as I want," I grumbled before mouthing, "Thank you," to Peter as he poured more coffee into my mug. He'd been with me for four years, and I wasn't sure what I'd do without him. I'd been damn lucky he decided to move to Indiana with me because he managed all the moving parts that it took to run my home. With the acreage I bought and how big I'd gone with the house, he definitely had his hands full.

"You may want to resist the urge to give me shit."

I took a quick sip before asking, "How come?"

"Because you definitely want to hear what I have to say."

I set my cup down and leaned back in my chair. "Okay, now you've got my attention. Why did you call?"

"I have a showing on the storefront where that boutique used to be."

My brows drew together. "Not sure why you thought I needed to know that. You show my commercial spaces in town all the time without giving me updates unless I need to sign a lease. Maybe I wasn't clear with you about this, but I wasn't planning on changing how we worked together when I moved here."

"Give me more credit than that, cuz. My meeting isn't with just *any* potential tenant this morning. I'm calling as your wingman, not your real estate broker. Unless you changed your mind about pursuing the gorgeous widow."

I shot out of my seat, almost knocking my coffee over in the process. "Skylar wants to lease commercial space from me?"

"She didn't say a peep about you when she called my office this morning. I don't think she realizes who owns the building."

"That's not what I asked," I growled.

He made a tsk-ing sound. "For a guy who's basically retired, you sure are wound up tight."

"Dean."

My cousin got the hint and finally answered my question. "Like I said, she's interested in the corner shop on Main and Union. She didn't tell me what kind of place she was hoping to open, but it's a prime location for just about any kind of business."

I knew the spot. The little boutique that had previously occupied the space had done quite well, but the owner opted not to renew her lease a few months ago. Her husband's employer had transferred him to the West Coast, leaving her without much choice. "Did she mention the office space above it?"

"No, that's a separate listing. I was going to let her know it's vacant during her tour this morning."

"Don't." My lips curved into a grin. "Take the listing for the office space down. I don't want to lease it out anymore. I'm going to use it myself."

"So much for being basically retired." He laughed, but I didn't take offense. It only made my smile widen. "I'm glad to hear that the way she took off after you asked her out didn't ding your confidence enough that you decided to back off."

"Not even a little bit," I assured him as I stalked out of the small dining room, heading upstairs to change.

"Then I guess I'll see you soon."

"Damn straight," I murmured as the call dropped.

A little more than an hour later, I parked my truck at the curb in front of the storefront Skylar was hoping to lease. As I climbed out of the vehicle, I looked through the tempered glass windows lining the front of the space. The woman who'd occupied much of my thoughts since we met was turning in a circle with a big smile on her beautiful face. Unfortunately, the excitement drained from her expression when she spotted me walking toward them. Her lips moved as her focus shifted to Dean, but I couldn't tell what she'd said. It was easy to guess when I yanked the door open and heard his answer. "Yes, I told him about this meeting, Skylar. He's my client."

"Your client?" she echoed, her nose scrunching as she shot me an accusing look. "You want to lease this space, too?"

I shook my head. "Nope. I own it."

"Yeah, that makes more sense than you wanting to rent it," she sighed, her shoulders slumping.

"Is that going to be a problem?" Dean asked.

"I think it would be best if you find another place." The disappointment in her eyes betrayed the confidence in her tone. She wanted this storefront. Leasing it from me was the problem.

Her reaction emboldened me. She wouldn't be fighting so hard if she was indifferent. With how quickly she'd turned me down when I'd asked her out, I thought I'd been wrong about the attraction being two-sided. But now I was fairly certain my first instinct had been right.

Leaning my hip against the counter, I crossed my arms over my chest. "Not on Main Street."

"Pardon me?"

The grin I flashed her was smug. "You'll be

wasting your time looking for a different option on Main Street unless you want to open up shop a few blocks away from all the foot traffic."

She dragged her gaze from me to ask Dean, "What is he talking about?"

"Although my cousin just moved to town, he's been buying commercial property in Mooreville for almost two decades." Dean shot me a glare for putting him in the position of having to be the one to break the news to Skylar. "He owns all the buildings on the main drag."

"All the buildings?" she echoed, her eyes going wide as her gaze darted back toward me.

"Yup." My smile widened as I nodded. "My first big investment was right across the street. I was only twenty-one and had just come into the trust fund my maternal grandparents had set up for me. My dad thought I was being foolish, wasting my money in a place like Mooreville. I proved him wrong. Property values may not increase as much as they do in New York, but the steady flow of income from tenants who never miss a payment combined with a lower entry cost and potential for future appreciation meant less risk for me. None of my deals in Moore-ville have gone south. They've all made me a tidy sum, much to his chagrin."

"Of course, they have." Her eyes were pleading as she stared up at Dean, and I had the strangest urge to knock him out of the way so she'd keep her focus on me instead. "There isn't anywhere else that would work?"

"For the kind of shop you want to open, this is your best option. You won't find another place with the kind of traffic counts that you'd get here, both vehicular and on foot," Dean explained.

She jerked her thumb in my direction. "And you're not just saying that because he's your cousin?"

He shook his head as he tapped the screen of his phone and turned it so she could see what he'd pulled up. "You don't have to take my word for it. I have all the data to back me up right here."

After doing a quick check of the numbers, she heaved a deep sigh and turned back toward me. "How involved do you plan on being with your tenants now that you live in Mooreville?"

"You can count on me taking a hands-on approach." The sensual undertone to my reply was impossible to miss, as was the flash of awareness in her blue orbs that she tried to hide from me.

"I should've known you'd say something like that," she muttered, walking over to the window to stare outside at the passersby.

"The lease terms Baxter offers to the people of Mooreville are quite favorable." Dean tapped his finger against the top of a stack of papers on the counter. "He's always been a big supporter of local commerce."

"I do have one minor change to the standard lease I've been using." I reached into the inside pocket on my suit coat and pulled out a pen. Sliding the lease documents closer, I flipped through them to the back page and started writing.

Skylar stormed over, her eyes narrowing as she hissed, "What are you adding?"

"Just one small, extra clause." Once I was done, I stepped back so she could read what I'd written.

"You're going to require business consulting with you as a clause in all of your leases?" I didn't understand the smile she beamed at me until she added, "That's sure to keep you busy with all of the buildings you own."

I shook my head. "Nope."

She slammed her palm down on the paperwork. "Then why are you making it a condition for me?"

We both damn well knew why I was pushing this, but she just didn't want to admit it. Quirking a brow, I asked, "Why are you arguing against this so hard? You're a first-time business owner, and I'm a highly successful real estate mogul. You should be jumping at the chance to learn from me."

She planted her hands on her hips, jutting out her chin. "And I would be, if I didn't know that you have an ulterior motive."

"My reasons shouldn't factor into your decision." I held my pen out to her. "Consider this lesson number one—never turn down free help from an expert."

She yanked the pen from my grasp. "Not even if it's a trap?"

"Even then," I confirmed with a nod. "Figure out a way to twist it to your advantage, babe."

"I have the utmost respect for your grandparents." She pointed the tip of the pen at me. "But you, sir, are an ass."

I shifted my stance. "Am I an ass who's going to get his way?"

"Yes, dammit."

The satisfaction I felt as she signed her name next to mine was just as much of a thrill as I felt when I inked a big deal. When she was done, I tapped my finger above the clause I'd added. "Don't forget to initial here."

While she muttered to herself about how impossible I was, I grinned at Dean over her head. He lifted his thumb in the air but dropped his arm when Skylar looked up and glared at him. "I'm not any happier with you than I am with your cousin."

He held his hands up in a gesture of surrender. "What did I do?"

"You should've let me know Baxter owned this place before I came to look at it," she grumbled as she set the pen down on the counter.

Dean's brows drew together as he pretended that he didn't have a clue why she'd care. "I'm sorry. I didn't realize it was going to make a difference to you. As long as the lease terms are favorable, most of my clients looking for a commercial location don't normally care who owns the building."

"I guess you couldn't have known," she conceded with a huff. "But you still should have mentioned he was going to show up while we were here."

"That's fair." He jerked his thumb toward me. "I promise to give you a heads-up if he's going to crash another one of our showings of a property he owns in the future."

Skylar rolled her eyes. "Gee, thanks. That means an awful lot to me when I'm hoping it'll be years before I need your services again."

"Next month, next year, a decade from now...my

promise stands." Dean's eyes were filled with humor as he met my gaze. "So keep that in mind, cuz."

Since he'd left himself a lot of wiggle room with how specific he'd worded his promise, it was easy for me to reply, "No worries. I won't ask you to go back on your word with Skylar."

"Thanks, man." Dean picked up the stack of papers, folded them in half, and tucked them into the inside pocket of his suit coat. "I'll send scanned copies of these to each of you later today."

"Thanks." The meaningful look he shot my way let me know he was aware that he had my gratitude for more than just the paperwork.

"I appreciate it." Skylar adjusted her purse strap and started to follow Dean toward the door.

"Not so quick." I wrapped my fingers around her wrist. "We're not done yet."

Her eyes narrowed as she looked at me over her shoulder. "You may not be done, but I've accomplished everything I set out to do this morning."

"Have you already forgotten the clause you just initialed?" I stroked over the inside of her wrist, enjoying the flutter of her pulse beneath my thumb. She was doing a good job of masking her reaction to me, but the little things kept giving her away. "You can tell me about your plans for this space over lunch."

She turned toward me, her voice firm as she announced, "I am not having lunch with you."

"Then we'll do coffee instead," I suggested with a smile.

She tugged her hand free and shoved it into her jacket pocket. "You're not going to let this drop, are you?"

"Not a chance."

My answer frustrated her so much, I could practically see the steam coming out of her ears. "Fine, we can go to the diner for a coffee."

"I've heard that Trattoria serves the best espresso and cappuccino in town." The little Italian bistro's atmosphere was also bound to be a fuck of a lot more romantic, but that reason would sway her in the wrong direction.

"You think you're so smooth." She wagged her finger at me. "Just remember, this isn't a date. It's a business meeting."

I worked hard to keep my satisfied smirk under control as I placed my palm on her lower back to guide her out of the store. "Call it whatever you want, so long as you sit across from me."

I couldn't believe Baxter finagled me into joining him at one of the most romantic restaurants in town. After how difficult it had been to turn him down when he asked me out, I had every intention of staying as far away from him as I could. But here I was, sitting across from him in a cozy corner booth for two. At least with the late morning sunlight streaming through the windows, the ambiance was much less intimate than it was at night.

Setting aside the menu the hostess had given me, I studied the man sitting across from me, trying to figure out why he'd pushed so hard to get me here. He couldn't be that hard up for female company with his looks. "Do you blackmail women into going on dates with you often?"

He settled back in his seat, stretching his arms out along the back of the booth as he arched a brow. "I thought you said this wasn't a date."

Crossing my arms over my chest, I muttered, "You know what I meant."

He inclined his head, acknowledging my point. "I wouldn't call this blackmail."

"What would you call it then?" I asked, strumming my fingers on the top of the table.

"More like...extortion."

I narrowed my eyes. "Nobody is going to press charges against you for either crime. You're splitting hairs so you can avoid the question."

"This is the first time I've extorted a woman into joining me for a cup of coffee." He traced his finger around the rim of his empty water glass. "Or anything else."

His answer shouldn't have mattered to me, but it did. "I guess I'm special then."

"Definitely," he confirmed with a nod. "I can't even remember the last time I was out on a date."

"Not a date." The reminder was for me as much as it was him. Despite my denials, this very much felt like a date.

"How about this?" His lips curved into a slight smile. "I can't remember the last time I had the pleasure of sitting across from a beautiful woman like this."

I quirked a brow and tilted my head to the side. "I find that difficult to believe."

"It's the truth." He did a little half-shrug. "Why are you so surprised?"

My chin dipped low as my feet shuffled beneath the table. "Sorry, I assumed billionaire bachelors went out with a different woman every week or something like that."

"You know what they say about assuming," he murmured.

Luckily, the server arrived at our table just in time to save me from putting my foot deeper in my mouth. "What can I get you?"

Baxter inclined his head to indicate that I should order first. "I'll just have a cappuccino please."

The server's pen flew over her notepad as he rattled off, "Please bring me an espresso, today's special focaccia, the meatballs and ricotta starter, an arugula and prosciutto wood fire pizza, and the zeppole for dessert."

When she walked away, I shook my head. "That's a lot of food for one person."

"I chose items that are easy to share, hoping to tempt you into eating something."

It was a smart plan, especially since he had picked several of my favorite dishes. But I wasn't willing to let him know that he'd won this battle. Not yet. "You're lucky I love their cappuccino, or else you never would've gotten me here."

"Don't underestimate my tenacity. I have every faith that I would have eventually worn you down."

His confidence was infuriating. And unfortunately, also sexy. It didn't help that I was flattered by his persistence. Every other guy I'd turned down had quickly moved on to someone else, but Baxter seemed to be stuck on me for some strange reason.

"I wouldn't be too sure about that if I were you. I can be fairly stubborn myself," I warned.

He flashed me a cocky smile. "Oddly enough, I like that about you. Even though my life would be a lot easier if you were more agreeable."

"I guess you'll just have to settle for the fact that I agreed to come here with you to discuss my business plan." I pulled a stack of papers out of my purse and slid them across the table. "I thought Dean might need this for the lease agreement, but he barely asked any questions once I confirmed the monthly rent was within my budget. You may want to talk to him about how he screens potential tenants for your properties."

"I'm sure that won't be necessary. He's normally quite thorough."

I narrowed my eyes at that little nugget of information, wondering if he'd talked to his cousin about me and that was why Dean had skipped some steps in his usual leasing process. The idea should've been outlandish, but Baxter was a billionaire—he could afford the loss if I defaulted on the lease.

"Mm-hmm," I hummed beneath my breath as the server dropped off our coffees and a basket with pesto and mozzarella focaccia. The bread smelled delicious, and I couldn't resist the temptation it presented. I lifted a slice to my lips, letting out a low moan of appreciation when the savory flavor burst across my taste buds.

Baxter set my business plan to the side and snagged a piece for himself. "It's good, huh?"

"Incredible," I mumbled after swallowing another bite.

With how adamant I'd been about only having a cappuccino, I would have understood if he gloated over his little victory. I was impressed that he only flashed me a small smile before devouring his piece of focaccia. We didn't talk much over the next twenty minutes as we worked our way through all the dishes he had ordered.

It wasn't until the server dropped off dessert that he reached for my business plan again. "Tell me about the shop you want to open."

"Leaves and Pages is going to be a combination tea room and book shop."

He nodded. "I like the name. It's catchy."

"Thanks." I smiled at him, touched more than I should have been by his approval.

"What made you want to combine the two?" he asked, turning to the next page of my plan.

"Tea and books are my favorite things, besides my son."

He jerked his chin at the cappuccino I'd finished in the middle of our meal. "And here I thought you were more of a coffee woman with how much you enjoyed your cappuccino."

"I usually limit my coffee to a cup in the morning to kick-start my day, but I can drink tea all day long. If I had to pick, I'd choose tea over coffee nine times out of ten."

"Duly noted."

The wrinkling of his nose made me laugh. "I'm guessing you're not a tea fan?"

One of his shoulders lifted in a casual shrug. "I'm definitely a coffee man."

"Maybe I'll be able to change your mind. Some dandelion root blends taste a lot like coffee."

He recoiled, his lip curling in disgust. "I'll pass on anything that comes from a noxious weed people yank from their lawns. And any tea I drink had better come fully loaded with caffeine. None of that herbal stuff for me."

I wasn't surprised he didn't like my suggestion. Most people didn't look at dandelions—let alone their roots—and think about how good they'd taste. They had a bad rap, even with a lot of tea drinkers. "Certain kinds of black tea have a rich malty flavor and lots of caffeine. You might like one of those instead."

"If you want to try to turn me into a tea drinker, I'm willing to give it a try." He smiled as he leaned back in his chair.

"Just so long as I don't try to trick you into drinking any dandelion roots." My cheeks filled with heat when I realized how flirtatious that had sounded.

Instead of pushing the advantage, Baxter asked, "What kind of books do you like?"

"All of them." I laughed at the skeptical quirk of his brow. "I used to work at the library, so reading across genres made me better at my job. If a patron came in looking for a science fiction or horror book, I wanted to be able to recommend something. After I left, I found myself still picking up stories that I wouldn't have read before my time at the library."

"It sounds as though you liked it there. Why did you leave?"

I tucked my hair behind my ear, crossing my legs beneath the table. "When Steven died, I wanted to be there for my son whenever he might need me. My job at the library wasn't very demanding, but I didn't want any outside distractions. It was a difficult time for both of us."

"I know they say not to make any major life decisions when you're struggling with grief, but losing someone important has a way of making you reevaluate your priorities."

I didn't know Baxter much better than I had when I'd brought him an apology cake, but I didn't feel the same awkwardness when his brother's death came up this time. I didn't have any siblings, but I remembered all too well how I'd felt when my world came crashing down around me. Stretching my arm out, I patted his hand. "Like packing up your life in New York to move to Mooreville?"

"Yeah, I've been told that I'd come to regret my knee-jerk response to Weston's death." His hands shook as he pushed the plate with his half-eaten zeppole away from him. "But he would have respected my decision. He was fifteen years younger than me but so much wiser. He was only twenty-one when he bucked our parents' expectations and dropped out of college to live his dream of becoming a firefighter."

The pain was evident in his voice, and there was a tortured gleam in his eyes. I swallowed past the lump in my throat to ask, "Your parents weren't happy with your choice?"

He sighed and shook his head. "Absolutely not. My dad couldn't wait to leave Mooreville behind him when he started college, and my mom hasn't stepped foot in this town in all the years they've been together. Neither of them understands what drew me here."

"How are they dealing with their loss?"

"I didn't just leave New York because of Weston's death. If my parents had handled things differently, I probably wouldn't have sold all my property there. But they made it impossible for me to be near them." A muscle jumped in his jaw. "When Weston died on duty, their first instinct was to rant about how they'd told him not to become a firefighter and if he'd just listened to them, he'd still be alive."

If anything ever happened to Simon, I wouldn't know what to do with myself. But one thing I did know was that I would bend over backward to do whatever it took to ensure he was happy and wanted me in his life. "I'm so sorry."

His chin dipped slightly. "I was lucky, though. I had the rest of my family to help me navigate through the loss of my brother. They rallied around me even though I hadn't done a good job of keeping in touch throughout the years."

"That's what family is for." I just wished mine was bigger because then Simon would have more people to rally around him if he ever needed it...and I wouldn't have been stuck with only Steven's parents to depend on in our darkest moment.

"Sorry, I'm getting awfully personal for a business meeting."

His apologetic smile kind of made me wish I hadn't insisted this wasn't a date. But that would've been the height of foolishness because I wasn't ready to get involved with anyone. Even if I was, jumping into the dating pool with Baxter would've been asking for my heart to be broken since the sexy billionaire was way out of my league.

"No worries. My business plan doesn't exactly make for riveting conversation."

"You're not giving yourself enough credit. You did a great job with this." He scooted the stack of papers in my direction. "What type of vibe are you hoping to achieve?"

After flipping through the pages, I tapped my finger against the pink and green logo I'd had designed. "I want the space to be unabashedly feminine. There will be lots of pink, live plants scattered throughout the store, and shelves of books everywhere. I want it to be a place where the people of Mooreville can come to press pause for a little bit. Leave the hectic pace of their lives behind while they enjoy a pot of excellent tea that will leave them feeling refreshed and restored. But I also wanted to incorporate my love of books, which is where the pages part comes in."

"Unabashedly feminine isn't exactly my style, but I see the appeal in what you want to create. Are you planning to host events?"

I nodded. "Absolutely. I'd love to host birthday parties, going all out on the tea party theme on the weekends."

"I'm sure they'll be quite popular with all the young girls in town." His expression softened. "Do you have a plan for the books you'll carry?"

I leaned forward, my words tumbling out. "Since

I'll only have so much room for them, they'll be carefully curated, with priority given to local authors."

"Are you thinking about doing events with them?"

"I would love to."

"Good, I'll talk to Silas. I'm sure he'll jump at the chance to support your shop."

Baxter's cousin was a bestselling thriller author. Any event he participated in was bound to be a big draw. "Really? Thank you. That would be amazing."

"Happy to help."

"I also want to have one of those little free libraries out front for used books that my customers want to share."

I'd expected him to be against the idea since giving away free books could cut down on my revenue, but he tilted his head as he considered it. "You should put it in the back of the shop, like grocery stores do with the milk to draw people in. Then they might buy a tea before leaving with their free book. Or even find something else on the shelves they'd prefer to read."

My mouth fell open slightly as I breathed, "That is diabolically smart."

There was a satisfied gleam in his eye. "I told you I'd be an asset to your business."

"That you did."

"Maybe I could be of even more help. Are you looking for investors?"

"No." I didn't like talking about Steven. I never quite knew what to say. He wasn't a bad person. He had just been a bad husband, only I hadn't known it at the time. "My husband was a little obsessive about life insurance."

A muscle jumped in his jaw. "As a firefighter with a wife and child, that was a smart call."

This part of the explanation was easier since it was focused on the positive. "I'm not sure why he kept so many policies after he was promoted to fire marshal, but it turned out to be a godsend in the end. Between the term life policy paying out double because it was an accidental death and the private mortgage insurance paying off our house, I was able to stay home with Simon when he needed me the most. And there's still more than enough left over to pay for his college education and launch my business."

"Then I guess I'll have to figure out some other way to become indispensable to you."

His statement sounded a bit like a threat...and I had a feeling he meant it as a promise.

Using the office above the shop that Skylar leased from me had seemed like the obvious move, but it hadn't yielded any results a week later. It seemed like I'd bumped into just about everyone else in Mooreville except for her. If she knew I was using the space, I might've become paranoid that she was avoiding me after our business lunch that had felt a whole lot more like a date. Even though she refused to think about the time we spent together as anything other than business, there was no denying that our conversation had taken a personal turn. Or that the attraction between us had grown.

I was still convinced that she'd eventually give in to our chemistry if we spent more time together...I just had to find her first. And not in a creepy stalker way or I'd just scare her off.

I'd popped into the office three times in the past week, but from the town gossip Dean had shared with me, Skylar had visited the shop on the two days I hadn't been there. I was hoping my luck would improve today. Unfortunately, as I drove past her storefront, the lights were off, and there was no sign of her car. Circling the building, I parked my Tesla in back and trudged inside. Even though I'd unloaded most of my properties in New York, I had more than enough tasks on my to-do list to keep me busy for at least a few hours.

Settling in the Herman Miller executive chair that had been delivered on Friday, I checked my email. The first message that caught my eye was from my dad. Instead of opening it, I logged into my accounts to manage my stock portfolio. It didn't take me long to lose myself in the numbers, for which I'd always had an affinity. My knack for math had given me an advantage in college, helping me graduate summa cum laude from Harvard during my undergraduate studies in quantitative economics and earning me a coveted Rhodes scholarship.

My parents were proud of my achievements, and my dad had been grooming me to take over my maternal grandfather's company when he was ready to step down. I'd leveraged my trust into the kind of wealth that meant my children's children—if I was ever lucky enough to have any—would be set for life. But my accomplishments weren't much comfort when Weston died. And neither was my mom and dad's approval.

Even though I'd worked with my dad since I was twenty-five, I hadn't been close to my parents. They'd never been hands-on with Weston and me growing up, leaving our care mostly to a succession of nannies. I'd tried to be there for my younger brother as much as I could, even with the sixteen years that separated us. My parents hadn't listened when I'd urged them to pay more attention to Weston than they had me. Or when I'd backed him on his decision to join the fire department—something they'd held against me after his death and drove us further apart.

About an hour later, I was finally thinking about reading my dad's email when my cell phone rang. Seeing the name on the screen, I grinned as I accepted the call. "Good morning, beautiful."

"Um. Hey, Baxter."

My smile widened at the breathiness in her voice. "How can I help you?"

"I was hoping you could meet me at the store sometime today. I have some plans for the renovations on the space that I wanted to run by you."

That was an offer I couldn't pass up. "Absolutely. What time works for you?"

"The sooner, the better since I'm working around Simon's schedule and I'm already here."

I glared at the door I'd shut behind me and made a mental note to leave it open from now on. Then I'd have a better chance at hearing her when she was downstairs. If she hadn't called me, I probably would have missed out on this golden opportunity to spend time with her. "Give me a couple of minutes, and I'll be right down."

"Right down?"

Her confusion was adorable. "Yes, I took over some open office I own downtown. I decided that it would be good for me to get out of the house more often, so I didn't become a recluse."

She proved she was as smart as I thought when after a short pause she asked, "Is the office you just so happened to decide to take over upstairs from my shop?"

"It is," I confirmed, smiling big enough that my cheeks started to hurt.

"And when did you come to the conclusion that you were at risk of turning into a hermit?" she asked.

"The same day you signed your lease." My answer gave a lot away, but I didn't mind. It wasn't as though I was trying to hide my interest in her.

She heaved a deep sigh. "I don't know what to do with you, Baxter Moore."

"I have quite a few suggestions that I'm more than willing to give you." And it went without saying that a fuck ton of them involved us getting naked.

She laughed. "I'm sure you do, but I'm going to ask you to keep them to yourself while you're down here looking over my plans for the build-out."

"As you wish." For now, at least.

"Uh-huh."

She sounded skeptical, but I couldn't blame her. It would be damn difficult to keep things professional with her. But that wasn't exactly what I'd promised to do. Asking her out was different than telling her what she could do naked in bed with me.

"Be there in a minute."

Just talking to her on the phone got me hard, and I had to adjust myself before I headed downstairs. The office I was using was a quick walk to Skylar's shop, and I found the back hallway door unlocked. Striding through it, I called, "Skylar?"

"Over here."

I followed the sound of her voice and found her standing on a step stool, trying to measure how tall the windows lining the front wall were. I raced across the room, placing one hand on the small of her back to steady her and reaching for the tape measure with the other. "Let me do that for you."

"Thanks. The tape measure was being a pain in my butt and wouldn't stay in place."

I waited until she stepped down to grumble, "Probably because you were trying to write down the numbers, perched on a step stool in heels, while taking the measurement all at the same time."

She ducked her head and mumbled, "I'm used to figuring out how to get things done by myself."

"Feel free to take advantage of me being upstairs whenever you want. I'm more than happy to help," I offered, looking over my shoulder to smile at her before taking the measurements she needed and calling out the numbers.

"All part of making yourself indispensable to me?" she muttered as she jotted down the dimensions of the window.

"It's a start." When I was done, I folded and picked up the stool before she could grab it. "Do you need anything else measured?"

"Nope, that's it. I have appointments with a few general contractors this week to discuss options for the build-out, but since they won't be handling the logo for the windows, I thought I'd get started on it while I'm picking out the team I want to work with."

She'd just given me the perfect opening to insert myself into the renovation process. "Since I'm paying for the build-out, I'd like to attend those meetings."

"I thought the renovation was supposed to be on my dime?"

"You're making capital improvements to commercial space that I own. It only seems fair that I foot the bill," I explained as I leaned the stool against the wall near the door to the back hallway.

Her eyes narrowed. "Is this another one of those special clauses that you slid into my lease agreement?"

"Tenant improvement allowances are pretty standard." I'd just been more generous with hers than I usually would be.

"But the actual build-out process is still controlled by me, correct?"

"Yes." Her smile faded when I added, "But with frequent updates provided to your landlord and regular site visits to check on the progress."

"And I suppose it's safe to assume that Dean won't be handling any of those visits as your agent?"

"Nope, I'll be doing those myself." I tapped my chest.

She sighed and shook her head. "I guess it's a good thing your new office is so close. It'll cut down on your commute."

"A lucky coincidence." I pressed my lips together to keep from smiling even though I wasn't fooling her at all.

"Mm-hmm." She walked over to the counter and yanked the rubber band off a rolled-up set of floor plans for the space. "This is what I asked you to come all this way to see."

Crossing the room to stand at her side, I peered down at the blueprints. I followed along while she explained her vision for the space, tracing her fingers over the areas she wanted to make the most changes. Her ideas were great, and I only had a few suggestions to offer. When she was done, I hated for my time with her to end. I'd been in hundreds of similar meetings on much larger projects but never enjoyed them as much. Her enthusiasm was contagious.

After rolling the plans back up, she tapped them

on the counter with a smile. "Thanks for all of your help."

I meant it sincerely when I replied, "It was my pleasure."

"I guess I'll see you tomorrow?" she asked, referring to the meeting with the first of the contractors on her list.

"I'll be here." I wrapped my fingers around her wrist when she turned to leave. "We could have lunch today, too."

She shook her head. "Sorry, but no."

I wasn't going to give up that easily. "Is tomorrow better for you?"

"I didn't say no because I was busy today."

"Why then?"

She tucked her hair behind her ear and broke eye contact with me. "We have nothing in common. I'm a small-town single mom, and you're a billionaire bachelor."

I pressed a finger under her chin, tilting her head back until she met my gaze again. "That's not true."

"Okay, name one thing we have in common," she challenged, balling her free hand into a fist and planting it on her hip.

With what I'd learned about her, it didn't take

me long to come up with something. "Neither of us is interested in dating."

She rolled her eyes and scoffed, "You asked me out on a date the second time we saw each other, blackmailed me into having coffee the next, and turned that into a full-blown lunch by tempting me with food I couldn't resist."

All of that was true, except I came to a different conclusion. "Good point. What I should have said was that neither of us was interested in dating until we met each other."

Her cheeks turned a pretty pink shade as she whispered, "Damn your confidence and charm."

Although I would've greatly enjoyed having lunch with her again, I had a feeling I'd lose what little progress I had made if I pushed too hard. Lifting my hands in a gesture of surrender, I murmured, "I'll back off for now, but please think about it."

She took the out I offered, whirling around to escape through the front door of the store. Our eyes met through the glass as she locked the door, and I continued to watch her as she walked to her car, captivated by the sway of Skylar's hips. As she pulled away from the curb, I was more determined than ever to convince her to give me a chance. If the attraction had been one-sided, I would have reluctantly backed off. But the sparks between us grew every time we were around each other...which meant that I needed to give us even more opportunities to bump into each other. And I had the perfect idea for how to make that happen while also giving Skylar a helping hand. Multitasking at its finest, with a little assistance from my cousin.

Stabbing my finger against the screen of my cell phone, I waited for Dean to pick up.

"Hey, Baxter. What's up?"

"I need your help as both my real estate agent and wingman."

"Double duty? I am definitely up for the task, whatever it may be."

I scanned the space, picturing the changes Skylar wanted to make. "I want the best team available working on the renovation for Skylar's shop."

"I must be better than I thought, and that's saying a lot because I've always known I was damn good. I already hooked her up with a great guy."

I growled at his choice of words.

His laughter drifted through the line before he said, "What I meant was I already gave her the name of a contractor who does great work on commercial build-outs."

"Do me a favor and give him a call tonight. Let him know that I'll make it more than worth his while to prioritize her project."

'Why are you in such a rush to make this happen?"

"The sooner the build-out is done, the sooner she can open the store." Then I could visit her there whenever I wanted. And I hadn't liked the catch in her voice when she'd said she was used to figuring out how to do things on her own. She deserved to have someone in her life who lent her a helping hand when she needed it...and I aimed to be that man for her.

# 8

SKYLAR

It was amazing what a difference a couple of months made. Between Dean's recommendations and Baxter's input, choosing a contractor had been easier than I'd expected. And the guy I'd gone with had worked wonders in bringing my vision to life.

As I walked through the space where my dream was becoming a reality, I was blown away by what had already been accomplished. When I was working on my plans, I thought it would take a minimum of six months before the place would be almost ready to open. But that was before Baxter had come into my life and shaken things up in a big way. He had more than fulfilled his promise to help get my project off the ground. And he'd become indispensable, just like he'd threatened.

The walls were painted a pale pink, with four rows of white oak shelves lining two of them. I'd swapped the boring LED drop ceiling lights with three oversized wood veneer ring chandeliers in a pale rose finish. A row of matching pendant lights hung over the counter and display case. The carpet had been torn out and replaced with a light engineered hardwood in a pale oak color. The open cabinets behind the counter were also a light oak, and the countertop was rose quartz.

The furniture I'd ordered was a mixture of pale oak, pinks, greens, and a light camel brown. A couple of pieces had already arrived and were sitting in the corner, and I could barely wait until the rest of it was here. The colors worked great together, and I'd definitely nailed the unabashedly feminine look I'd been aiming for.

I whirled around at a loud knock on the door. My best friend Sarah waved at me through the glass. Rushing over, I opened the door and greeted her. "Hey, what are you doing here?"

She gave me a quick hug before moving past me into the store. "I was driving past and saw your car out front. I thought I'd stop by to see how things were shaping up."

I swept my hand through the air and grinned. "As you can see, I am way ahead of schedule."

Her eyes were wide as she turned in a circle, taking in all the progress we'd made. "Holy crap, I can't believe how fast the renovation is moving. I thought you said you weren't going to be ready to even think about opening until closer to summer break?"

"I'm still going to wait until after school lets out to do a big opening. But I might do a trial run with shorter hours for a few weeks first."

"Like a friends and family thing?"

"Definitely a friends thing," I murmured with a grimace. Although Steven's parents made it a point to do something with Simon every couple of weeks, we hadn't really spent much time together since his death except for holidays. And my parents weren't due for a visit until after the store would be open.

"Rest assured, this friend"—she pointed at herself—"will be ready whenever you are."

"You better be." I laughed and shook my head as I pointed at the display case next to the counter. "I'm counting on you for all the baked goods I'm going to sell."

"Only until this place really takes off," Sarah reminded me. She was amazing in the kitchen and made eight of the top ten best desserts I'd ever tasted. Since she was self-taught, she tended to downplay her skills. But she'd built a nice little side business baking custom order cakes over the past couple of years, including a stunning three-tier baseball-themed one for Simon's fifteenth birthday. I couldn't wait to see what she did for him next month.

I'd had to do a heck of a lot of convincing to get her to agree to supply me with the treats to go along with my teas. She'd only been willing to commit to a trial run, convinced that I could do better with a commercial bakery. Figuring she wouldn't be able to deny how amazing she was when my clientele raved over her baked goods—because I had no doubt they would love them—I'd jumped at the chance to prove her wrong. "We'll see."

I wasn't surprised when she changed the subject back to the renovation. "But seriously, how did you manage to get so much done in so little time?"

"I can't take much of the credit. All I did was leave the work in capable hands."

"Capable hands, huh?" She wagged her brows. "Does your contractor have a crush on you? Please tell me he asked you out, and you didn't shoot him down right away like you have everyone else."

My cheeks heated as I shook my head. "Sorry, there's absolutely no chance for romance there. He's in his late fifties and happily married."

"Skylar Marie Hicks." She planted her fists on her hips. "You better tell me what that blush means. Fess up. Right now."

I bit my bottom lip, feeling nervous because I'd put off telling her about Baxter for far too long. We didn't keep secrets from each other, but with the hecticness of the past couple of months, we hadn't had a girls' night out in a while. Since we had a hard and fast rule that all of our girl talk—otherwise known as gossip since it usually wasn't about us—happened away from the kids, I'd been able to avoid this conversation. But that was only because Sarah had no idea anything had happened beyond Baxter asking me out when I'd brought him an apology cake, him owning the building we were currently standing in, and that we'd gone to Trattoria to discuss the lease—which she'd heard through the grapevine and asked me about.

"So...you know how I mentioned that Baxter Moore was my landlord?"

Sarah quirked a brow. "I take it that the sexy billionaire really came through for you?"

"I didn't say he was sexy." At least not out loud.

"You didn't have to. I've heard plenty about the newest Moore in town from all the other single women in Mooreville." She flashed me a bemused smile. "If your vagina wasn't full of cobwebs that you never planned to clear out, you would've been the one to tell me how hot he is."

"I cannot believe you just said that." I was used to her bluntness, but that was a lot, even for her.

She ignored my complaint and carried on with her rant. "Those same women were all in a tizzy over your little tête-à-tête with him. If I thought it would do any good, I would've figured out a way to set the two of you up together weeks ago. Nobody in this town deserves a sexy billionaire boyfriend more than you. And he couldn't do any better than you. But I learned my lesson on trying to play matchmaker with you. Even though it's killing me inside."

I tugged at the collar of my shirt, my voice cracking as I said, "I know it does. Thank you."

"Oh, my gosh!" She pumped her fist in the air. "Something is going on with you and Baxter, isn't there?"

Sarah wasn't one to whisper, and today was no

exception. Lifting my index finger to my lips, I shushed her. "Shh, he might hear you."

"How?" She glanced around the store as though she expected to spot him somewhere.

I pointed at the ceiling. "He's using the office upstairs."

"He really isn't trying to hide his interest in you at all, is he?"

It was too late to try to deny anything, so I just shook my head and sighed, "Not even a little bit."

She stomped over to the back door and flipped the lock. Then she pulled her phone out of her back pocket, pulled up a playlist, and put the volume at one of the loudest settings before placing the device on the counter. Once that was done, she grabbed me by the elbow and led me into the back room, where there was a small walk-in refrigerator. Dragging me inside, we were squished together when she slammed the door shut behind us. "There, he can't hear us now. Tell me everything."

"It's freezing in here," I protested, rubbing my arms with my hands in an attempt to stay warm.

She tapped her foot on the metal floor. "Then I guess you'd better talk fast."

I heaved a deep sigh before it all came spilling out.

"He's asked you out how many times?"

I tucked my hair behind my ear. "A dozen. Maybe more. At first, he asked pretty much every time he saw me. But he slowed down once the renovation started."

Her eyes widened. "Is that disappointment I hear in your voice?"

"I don't know. Maybe." My gaze bounced around the inside of the cooler. "I guess I got used to him asking, and the first time he didn't, I thought he wasn't going to ask again. And I was confused because I would've still said no, but I liked being asked. By him, at least. Even though we kind of sort of see each other a lot since he's involved himself in pretty much every step of the renovation. And he brings me a cappuccino from Trattoria at least once a week. I keep telling him he doesn't have to, but he doesn't seem to care. He just says he knows I like them, and it's a little thing he can do to brighten my day, so why shouldn't he? And I can never come up with a good reason...probably because I like them even more than usual because it's so darn thoughtful."

Sarah was standing completely still, with her arms hanging loosely at her sides. "I cannot believe you haven't told me any of this until now."

I could've blamed it on how busy we'd both been, but she deserved the truth—even if it was difficult to admit to myself. "I couldn't. If I had, it would've made the whole thing more real. And I wasn't ready for that."

"How about now? Are you finally willing to admit you're interested in him?"

I squeezed my eyes shut and took a couple of shallow breaths. "I think I just used up all my courage telling you what's happened so far. I'm not ready to think about what might come next."

"Okay, Skylar."

Her voice was gentle, and my eyes popped open when I heard the cooler door open. I heaved a sigh of relief as we stepped out and walked back over to the display case. After she turned the music off, I pointed at the empty shelves. "How about we discuss all of the delicious baked goods you're going to supply me with when Leaves & Pages opens? I made sure there was plenty of room because they're bound to be big sellers."

Her eyes were filled with understanding as she nodded. "You know I can't resist talking about my baking."

I flashed her a wobbly grin. "I know, that's what I was counting on."

"Fine," she huffed. "I'll let it go for now."

Some of the tension drained from my body. "Thank you."

Crouching low, she peered at the shelves inside the display case. "That really is a lot of space."

"I wanted to make sure we had room to grow since it would be a pain in the butt to have a different display case put in later. Plus, I wasn't sure what all you had in mind."

"I thought we could start out with a variety of scones, muffins, cookies, and sweet breads. And maybe we could do some pairings," she suggested.

"Oh, I like that idea." I rubbed my hands together. "If you send me a list of the flavors you want to make, I'll look through my tea options and come up with a few combinations that pair well together."

She nodded. "Sure, I can do that tonight."

Her quick agreement was a relief. Since I was ahead of schedule on the remodel, I was anxious to get to work on perfecting the menu. "Great. I really appreciate your faith in me."

She tilted her head back to look up at me. "I think I should be the one saying that to you. All I'm going to be doing is baking some stuff. You're the one who's taking all the risks."

"You're seriously underestimating how awesome your baked goods are. If this place is a success, it's going to be in large part because people are going to be craving the stuff you're supplying me with, and they can't get them anywhere else."

She blushed at my compliment and stood, taking my hands in hers. "You're such a great friend."

"And you're the best friend I could ever ask for."

She squeezed my hands. "Which is why I have to tell you how happy I am that you finally met a guy who has your heart talking to your stubborn head."

"Sarah," I whispered, my voice trembling.

"You've been doing everything for others for the past five years. No"—she slashed her hand in the air —"make that fifteen years. It's past time you do something or someone for yourself."

"I like the new digs, but they don't compare to that corner office you used to have."

When Rigden had asked me to invest in his distillery, he had insisted that I didn't give him any special treatment just because he was family. He sent me his business plan, and after I had reviewed it and assured him that his plan was solid, he flew out to New York to pitch me in person.

Standing, I jerked my thumb over my shoulder and laughed. "How come? You don't like this view as much as my last one?"

"Nothing against Mooreville's town square, but those floor-to-ceiling windows overlooking the Brooklyn Bridge can't be beat."

"Not gonna argue with you there, but there are definitely other perks to being here."

"You mean the beautiful owner of the tea shop going in downstairs?"

I was going to have to get used to my family members poking their nose into my business more than usual. Not that my mom hadn't done her best when I lived in Manhattan. But she was only one person. Now that I had moved, a whole slew of relatives was interested in what I was up to. "It definitely doesn't hurt that I get to see Skylar just about every day."

Rigden dropped onto the chair in front of my desk. Stretching his legs out, he crossed his arms over his chest. "Is she why you're spending so much time here? I thought you had decided you were going to work less now that you don't have that high-stress job anymore."

"She's part of it," I conceded. "But I also quickly realized that I get bored very easily when I have too much time on my hands. There's only so much golfing I can do to keep me busy."

"Yeah, I can see how it would be rough going from sixty-hour workweeks to having nothing on your calendar." I didn't trust the mischievous gleam in his eyes. "And Skylar is one hell of a motivator. In fact, I'm thinking about asking her if she'd like to offer some spiked teas in her new shop when it opens. Not only would it be good for business since she has a primo spot on Main Street but working with her would give me a great excuse to spend some time with her."

I had no rights over Skylar. Although the chemistry between us was impossible to miss, she hadn't given in to it. Yet. But logic didn't seem to apply when it came to her, and I didn't like the idea of my very single cousin spending time with her when mine was limited. Even if it would be good for both of their businesses. "How hard is it to get a liquor license around here?"

Rigden laughed and shook his head. "Really? You can't come up with a better excuse than that? You know damn well that she'd have no problem getting one if I was the one supplying the alcohol. We're related to half the members of the town council."

I narrowed my eyes. "I thought you weren't a fan of nepotism?"

"Are you always gonna give me shit for wanting to do things the right way?"

"Probably." I smirked at him.

"Did it never occur to you that my approach gave me a free trip to New York City and confirmation from a well-respected businessman that my business plan was solid?"

"Did it never occur to you that you were always more than welcome to come for a visit, and I was more than happy to give you whatever advice you needed?" I retorted with a quirk of my brow.

His smug grin disappeared. "You got me there, man."

After our little verbal back-and-forth, my brain refocused on his suggestion. "I like your idea."

"Why do I hear a but in there?"

"I think I should be the one to make the pitch to Skylar."

He cocked his head to the side. "I didn't think silent partners made pitches?"

"Just remember, turnabout is fair play," I warned, strumming my fingers on my desktop. "When you find a woman, my conscience will remain clear while I give you exactly how much shit you decide to toss my way over Skylar."

He grimaced. "Shit, good point. I guess I should get to the real reason I stopped by."

"And that is?"

"I wanted to give you a heads-up about your dad."

That was the last thing I expected him to say. "What kind of a heads-up?"

"He's been calling my dad a hell of a lot more than he ever has before."

"That wouldn't take much." Rigden's dad was the second oldest behind mine. I wouldn't call them close, exactly, but it was the relationship my dad put the most effort into besides his parents. But by effort, I meant that he called his brother on his birthday and major holidays. "Do you have any idea what they've been talking about?"

Rigden pointed at me. "You."

"Yeah, I assumed that was a safe guess. But what about me in particular?"

"Your dad seems pretty damn sure that you're going to regret your decision and come crawling back to the East Coast and his company."

Leaning back to stare at the ceiling, I heaved a deep sigh. "He doesn't understand, and he never will."

"Does it matter either way?" Rigden asked.

I shook my head. "Not really. I've already made my decision, and there's no going back for me."

"As happy as I am to have you here, it would be wrong of me not to point out that there actually is."

"I didn't mean it that way." I sat up and met his gaze. "I'm happy with the choice I made. I like being in Mooreville even though it's different from what I'm used to."

"Good, I like having you around." He nodded. "Enough that I'm willing to make an exception to the silent bit of our partnership this one time only. You can talk to Skylar about my idea. Let me know if she wants to move forward with it."

"Will do." I stood and headed for the door. "

"I guess I'll head that way and say hello on my way out." When I slid him a suspicious glance, he chuckled. "I swear, I'll be there for a minute, tops."

"Fine," I grumbled as I led him down the stairs and through the door that nobody but Skylar and I used.

"Hey, Skylar. Nice to see you," Rigden greeted, taking in all the changes that she'd made. "I like what you did with the place."

"Thanks." She returned his smile before her gaze landed on me. "I owe a lot of thanks to your cousin for how smoothly everything has gone."

Rigden clapped me on the back. "He has something he needs to talk to you about that will hopefully be as helpful as his assistance with the build-out has been."

"You do?" she asked, tilting her head to the side.

"I'll leave you two to it." He grinned and gave me a thumbs-up behind Skyler's back before turning on his heel to head out the front door.

Skylar's brows drew together at Rigden's quick exit. "That sounded awfully mysterious."

"He actually had a really great idea about mixing his liquor with your tea to offer some special drinks when you open. If you approve, I can get working on the liquor license. It shouldn't be too hard to pull some strings and make it happen before you open."

"Tea cocktails with alcohol from a local distillery are a great idea, but I'm not a big drinker." Her nose wrinkled. "I probably wouldn't be great at coming up with recipes to use."

"You're familiar with tea, and I know Rigden's liquor. If we put our heads together, I'm sure we can come up with a few options that'll work," I suggested.

She looked over her shoulder at the canisters of tea she'd placed on the shelves behind the counter. "I was actually thinking about taking some of the blends I'm not that familiar with home, but maybe we could do a little tasting now instead? Maybe you'll be inspired."

I was thrilled to have her all to myself, even if it meant I had to choke down some tea. "You're not going to make me drink that dandelion stuff you mentioned, are you?"

She laughed and shook her head. "No, I have a small amount in stock for the diehard tea fans, but I don't want to scare you off."

I held her gaze so she could see how serious I was when I said, "I don't think there's much you could do to scare me off."

Her expression softened as she murmured, "The things you say."

"They're all true."

Her, "I'm starting to think they are," was so soft that I almost didn't hear it. I did, though. But I didn't push her to explain because she burst into a flurry of activity that let me know she wasn't ready to discuss it yet. Her admission had confirmed her protective walls were starting to weaken around me, and that was enough of a victory. For now, at least.

I kept our conversation light as she heated water and brewed ten kinds of tea. When she took down twenty cups and lined them in two rows, I laughed and shook my head. "I never thought I'd see the day when I would happily participate in a tea tasting."

Her gorgeous blue eyes had a mischievous glint as she smiled at me. "Should I get a spit bucket? Like they do for wine tasting."

I shook my head. "As long as you don't try to sneak that dandelion crap in, I think I'll be okay."

Whirling around, she grabbed another tin from the shelf and handed it to me. "Here, you can hold this, just in case I can't resist the temptation."

"Good idea," I murmured.

I studied her movements as she filled our cups halfway full with the different flavors she'd selected. She was so graceful, I could have happily stared at her all day.

When she had everything set up, she stayed on her side of the counter and nudged the cup on the far left toward me. "This one's Earl Grey. After our conversation about which kind of tea coffee drinkers might like best, I did a little research. It's the safest bet."

I lifted my cup to hide my satisfied smirk. There was no way in hell anyone would be able to convince me she'd looked into the kind of tea I'd be most likely to enjoy for any other reason than she'd been thinking about serving it to me. After taking a sip, I admitted, "Not too bad."

"How about this one? It's an Irish breakfast that's pretty robust."

I discovered I liked that one as well, along with a few others. And I'd been happy to find several options for cocktails. After I'd jotted down some notes about the Earl Grey, orange spice, and cinnamon teas that I thought would pair well with Rigden's gin, rum, and rye whiskey, I noticed the considering gleam in Skylar's eyes. I assumed she was thinking about the cocktails, so she surprised me when she asked, "You're Mooreville's most eligible bachelor. How come some amazing woman hasn't already snatched you up?"

I was encouraged by the fact that she was asking about my dating life. And had apparently talked to her best friend about me. Hopefully, it meant she was starting to think of me as more than just her landlord. "I know it's a cliché, but I was married to my work. I've never even come close to popping the question to anyone."

"Clichés are clichés for a reason." She pressed her lips together, her shoulders slumping.

I reached across the counter to interlace our

fingers. "And now you've given me another reason to be glad that I left all that behind me in New York."

Her hand trembled beneath mine. "You barely know me."

"I know that you're as beautiful on the inside as you are on the outside, which is saying a fuck of a lot with how damn gorgeous you are. You're also smart, loyal, and kind. The total fucking package." And I was willing to wait however long it took to make her mine.

Almost all of the remaining furniture had been delivered and set up in the past week. This morning, my first order of books arrived, and I'd barely made it five minutes before I started unpacking them. Sitting cross-legged on the floor, I appreciated my decision to wear jeans and a sweatshirt today because cutting open boxes was dirty work. I'd used my outfit to wipe the cardboard dust from my hands several times, and I probably had some in my hair too since I had fixed my ponytail when it'd started slipping.

I was a mess, but that didn't stop me from smiling when Baxter rapped his knuckles against the back door as he walked through it. Now that I had inventory in my shop, I probably should've started to keep it locked when I was here by myself—which was most of the time—but I didn't want to give him a reason to think his visits were unwanted. I liked how he popped in to see me whenever we were in the building at the same time.

"Hey, beautiful." He flashed me a sexy grin as he strode over to where I was sitting and stretched his arm out.

I accepted the to-go drink with a smile. "You don't have to bring me a cappuccino when you come to see me."

"You know I like to brighten your day."

My heart melted at the sincerity in his voice. He'd said the same thing often, but I was only recently starting to understand how much he meant it. "You don't need to come bearing gifts to make that happen. Just bring yourself."

"Whenever and wherever you want," he promised as he dropped down the floor next to me, stretching his long legs out instead of crossing them. "Just say the word, and I'll be there."

"I'll keep that in mind," I whispered.

He scanned my expression, and his smile widened. "Good."

When he reached into the box nearest to him, I shook my head. "You don't need to help with these.

I'm having a lot of fun going through the books I've ordered and thinking about how I want to display them. And you're not exactly dressed for the mess all of this entails."

Although Baxter left the big city behind him, he tended to dress as though he was still there. Not that I had any complaints. He filled out his suits as though they'd been made for him. Which they probably were. And they most likely cost a pretty penny, too.

It was money well spent, as far as I was concerned. I had dreamed about stripping him out of them more often than I cared to admit. Ever since Sarah tried to get me to admit I was interested in Baxter, I hadn't been able to get him out of my head. It was like she'd flipped a switch in my brain that gave me permission to think of him as a potential boyfriend—or lover, or whatever women in their mid-thirties called the men they dated. I'd been out of the loop for too many years to know how new relationships worked anymore.

"I wouldn't want to take away from your enjoyment." He got to his feet, and I shamelessly stared at his butt when he turned to look at the changes to the shop since he'd last been here a few days ago. "The place is really coming together."

I smiled because he seemed to have learned how to back off just when I needed him to and was surprised to discover that his insight into what I was feeling didn't scare me as much as it used to. It was even a little comforting that he'd come to know me so well. "It isn't too pink for you?"

"I have to admit, I wasn't sure I'd feel comfortable here when you described the vibe as unabashedly feminine." He trailed his fingers along the back of a camel-colored leather chair. "But the furniture you picked out is sturdy enough that I won't need to worry about breaking it."

"Give it a whirl," I suggested, jerking my chin toward the chair as I stood. "It'll definitely hold you."

He sat down and settled in, crossing his ankles and resting his elbows on the armrests. "I hope you're planning on your customers not wanting to leave because this is comfortable as fuck."

"I'm counting on it." I rubbed my hands together. "The longer they stay, the better the odds that they'll spend more money."

He flashed me an approving grin. "I like the way you think."

"Let's hope the customers do, too."

"Can you give me the contact information for the company you bought these from?" He leaned his head back and squeezed the armrests. "I think I want one for myself."

I did a double take, my eyes going wide. When I popped into his office last month, I recognized the chair behind his desk from a magazine. The ergonomic executive chair was a similar shade to the one he was sitting in, but that was where the similarities ended. The one he'd bought cost about five times what I paid for mine. "You like it that much?"

"You have excellent taste."

His approving grin sent butterflies swirling in my belly. "You can have that one. I'll even help you move it upstairs to your office."

"I'm not taking one of your chairs."

"You're not taking it. I'm giving the chair to you." I jiggled the cappuccino I'd been slugging back while we were talking. "You give me stuff to brighten my day all the time. Why can't I do the same for you?"

He patted the arms of the chair before standing. "There's a big difference between the coffee I bring you and a piece of furniture you bought for your store."

"Not when you factor in the overly generous build-out allowance you put into my lease that made it possible for me to up my furnishings budget in the first place." I swept my arm in a circular motion in front of me. "The shop wouldn't look nearly as good if it weren't for you. Giving you a chair seems like the least I can do."

He considered what I said before nodding. "I'll take it, but only if you let me show my gratitude by taking you to lunch."

My conversation with Sarah had been on my mind for the past couple of weeks, her final words replaying in my head over and over again. I hadn't wanted to admit that she was right because that would mean I needed to take a long, hard look at why I kept turning Baxter down on his offers. But she had made a good point. It was past time for me to think about living for myself, not just Simon. And I couldn't deny that my heart yearned for me to say yes even though my head kept reminding me why getting into a relationship was a bad idea.

I must have taken too long to respond because Baxter held his hands up in a gesture of surrender. "Never mind, beautiful. If you have to think about it that hard, then you aren't ready yet. I understand."

"Do you?" I asked with a sigh. "Because I don't."

He tilted his head to the side. "What don't you understand?"

"Why it's getting harder and harder to say no to you," I confessed.

"Maybe that's because you're supposed to be saying yes instead," he suggested with a small smile.

Baxter had put the past couple of months to good use. I had watched him prove how dependable he was. Week in and week out, he showed up for me. Solving problems before I knew they existed. I paid attention to how he brought me cappuccinos because he knew I liked them. Watched him try a variety of teas even though he didn't like them, just because it meant something to me. Not to mention how he had helped my son achieve his dream before he knew who we were. I had seen for myself that he didn't toss money at problems to make them go away. He gave his time and energy too. And not once had his interest in me wavered. I wouldn't have been able to blame him if it had, considering I had put him through the wringer with no guarantee of a payoff in the end.

"I think you might be right," I conceded, my voice wavering as I threw caution to the wind.

"Yeah?"

"Yes." This time my tone was firm. "But I don't want to go to Trattoria this time."

"Anywhere you want to go is more than fine by me. You name it, and I'll take you there."

I had a feeling that if I told him I wanted to see

the Eiffel Tower, he would whisk me off to Paris in a heartbeat. Knowing the lengths he would go to for me made it easier to accept the decision I had already made. "I don't have anywhere specific in mind. My only preference is that I am not ready for us to be out in public together on a date. I really don't want the whole town to gossip about us. At least not until we figure out where this is going, and I figure out if I need to talk to Simon about us. The last thing I want is for him to hear about us dating from someone else, and he already asked me about you after we went to Trattoria."

He moved close and gripped my hands with his. "I'm not going to be mad at you for being the kind of woman who protects her kid. That's a huge part of what drew me to you in the first place."

I appreciated his understanding and liked that he was okay with me being a mom first and a single woman second. "Thank you."

"No, thank *you* for giving me a chance." The squeeze of his hands sent a zing of awareness through my body.

My cheeks heated at the sincerity shining from his gray eyes. Although he had been blatant in his pursuit of me, I felt a feminine thrill at this further proof of him wanting me. "Don't thank me yet. Our first date could be a disaster. I haven't been on one in forever."

"Then it's a good thing for you that we've already gone out together before." He brushed his thumb over my knuckles. "There's no need for first-date jitters."

I laughed and shook my head. "I told you that wasn't a date."

He flashed me a playful grin. "Deny it all you want, but we shared a meal that I paid for in a romantic restaurant. Typical date stuff."

I wanted to argue since I'd been so entrenched in denying what had been going on with us, but I needed to move past that protective impulse if I wanted this to work. "Then I guess you better come up with something good for our next date since our first one went so well."

He quirked a brow. "Dinner tomorrow night?"

"How about lunch instead?" I suggested. "Simon would have questions if we went out to dinner, and I don't want to have to lie to him."

"I can work with lunch. Do you want to go now?"

He started to tug me toward the door, almost as though he thought I'd change my mind at any minute. I dug my heels in as I asked, "Don't you need time to plan?"

"I already have plenty of ideas." He tapped his index finger against his temple. "Over the past couple of months, I've done a lot of thinking about how I would woo you if given the chance."

How in the heck could he be so darn alpha and sweet at the same time?

## 11

I couldn't remember the last time I had gone all out planning a date for a woman. It was probably back in high school before I'd shot up past six feet tall and put on some muscle. Once I'd gotten past the awkward teenage phase, I hadn't needed to do much to attract female attention. But Skylar was different —and not just because she made me work for it. She was more than worth the effort I had put into our lunch over the past day.

A part of me had wanted to push harder for her to go out with me yesterday. After waiting so long, I was impatient for our first official date. But the last thing I wanted was to scare Skylar off when I'd finally convinced her to take a chance on me. Which was the only reason I'd agreed to her request to drive herself to my home instead of letting me pick her up.

I highly doubted we'd do more than eat the picnic I'd organized, but I still gave most of the household staff the afternoon off. Skylar had said she wanted to keep our date to ourselves, and even though my employees signed non-disclosure agreements that prevented them from speaking about my private life, I thought she'd prefer the added privacy.

I left the gate open and went out to wait on the front porch. At five minutes past noon, I started to wonder if she was going to try to bail on me—which would've meant that I needed to track her down—but then her car made the turn onto my property. A rush of triumph surged through my veins as I watched her pull to a stop in front of my house. Hurrying down the steps, I circled her vehicle to open her door. The startled pleasure in her eyes bothered me, and I was going to do my best to get her to the point where she grew accustomed to me doing little things for her.

"Hey, beautiful."

"Were you waiting for me?" Helping her from the car, I nodded. "I'm sorry I'm late."

"You can't really call five minutes late. It's more

like making an entrance even though you don't need any help with that."

"I almost didn't come," she admitted softly, ducking her head.

I slid my hand down her arm to interlace our fingers. "I know."

She looked up, and a wrinkle appeared in the middle of her brow. "How could you possibly know?"

"It took me two and a half months to talk you into a date. I figured it was safe to assume you'd get cold feet. That was why I was worried about giving you too much time to change your mind," I explained as I led her into the house. "What finally tipped the scales in my favor?"

Her head swiveled from the right to the left as she surveyed the entryway to my home. "I called my best friend for a pep talk."

I'd been expecting her to say something along the lines of not wanting to let me down after she gave me her word, but her answer was even better. If her best friend was on my side, that boded well for me. "Remind me to thank her for advocating in my favor."

"Sarah is a fan of Trattoria's tiramisu." Skylar tilted her head back and winked at me. "Just in case you need a suggestion for a thank-you gift since you're so big on giving people things to brighten their day."

"A slice of dessert isn't nearly enough for giving you a nudge in my direction." I pursed my lips and looked up as I pretended to consider a more appropriate gift for her friend. "Maybe a trip to Italy. There's a small, tucked-away eatery not too far from the Colosseum that serves the best tiramisu in the world."

Her spurt of laughter made me feel as though my heart was expanding in my chest. I wanted to hear it bouncing around the walls of my home on a regular basis.

"Don't repeat that offer in front of Sarah. Knowing my best friend, she'd run home to grab her passports so you could book the tickets."

"She wouldn't need her passport number until the pilot filed the manifest if I flew her private. That can happen as late as an hour before the flight, so she could just pack a bag while she's at it."

Skylar shook her head. "You definitely can't joke about that with her. Sarah would lose her mind about flying on a private plane to Chicago, let alone Rome."

"Who said I was joking?"

I could practically hear the wheels turning in her head while I led her to the kitchen so I could pull the picnic basket out of the refrigerator. As we headed toward the French doors leading to the patio, she asked, "Where are we having lunch?"

"I couldn't think of anywhere we'd be less likely to attract attention than my backyard."

When I opened the door for her, she gasped. "And what a yard it is. How much land do you have?"

"Just under one hundred acres." Seeing her stunned expression, I added, "I'm surprised the grapevine didn't report the number."

She shrugged. "I try not to pay too close attention to gossip."

Considering trading rumors was a favorite pastime in Mooreville, I was impressed with her answer. But not surprised because Skylar was one of the kindest people I'd ever met. From what I'd seen, she didn't have a mean bone in her body.

"I set everything else up over there." I pointed toward the blanket spread out on the lawn to our right. Pillows and cushions were stacked on one edge, lanterns on two corners, an umbrella for shade, a low table with place settings, silverware, linen napkins, and wineglasses.

She pressed her free hand against her chest. "Wow, it's so romantic."

I hadn't blushed since I was a kid, but her compliment made my cheeks heat. "I'm glad you like it."

"It's a good thing I didn't go with a skirt," she murmured as she got comfortable on the blanket.

I set the basket next to the low table before sitting down across from her. "You wouldn't have gotten any complaints from me about the view if you had."

She laughed softly, shaking her head. "Uh-huh, I'm sure you wouldn't."

I started pulling items out of the basket. A bottle of white sangria, ginger peach iced tea, sliced fruit, grilled vegetables, cheese, a salad with strawberries and feta, caprese skewers, a selection of sliced meats, olives, crackers, chicken panini sandwiches, and a box of chocolate truffles.

Skylar's eyes widened as I unpacked the food and drinks. "I have to admit, I'm pleasantly surprised."

I glanced at the spread I'd laid out. "I may have gone slightly overboard."

"Just a little bit." She leaned forward to start pulling lids off the containers. "But I like how you woo. It shows that you really did put as much thought into this as you said. And the iced tea is a particularly nice touch."

"I know how much you enjoy your tea and wasn't sure you'd want wine since you said you're not much of a drinker." I poured two glasses from each bottle. "But I told my chef to skip the brandy in the sangria, so there isn't a lot of alcohol in it."

"You have a chef," she echoed, her gaze drifting toward the house.

I wasn't sure why she was stuck on that point when I had a slew of staff around the house and on my property. "I do."

A light blush crept up her neck as her nose scrunched. "I feel kind of silly that I made you a chocolate sheet cake when you have a chef. It isn't very fancy, but at least I used a real recipe. Most of my baking comes from a box mix. When I even bother. It's so much easier just to ask Sarah to bake for me since her stuff is better than anything I could get from a bakery. But after the way I put my foot in my mouth, having someone else bake your apology cake seemed wrong."

She was so damn sweet. And so was the cake she made for me. "I'll have you know, I ate every single bite of that chocolate sheet cake."

Twisting a lock of hair around a finger, she murmured, "Then maybe I should make you another one some time."

"I'd love that." As great as the cake had been, I liked the idea that she was thinking about doing something for me in the future even more.

Our conversation flowed smoothly as we made a dent in the mountain of food I'd asked my chef to prepare. Leaning back on a stack of pillows with a soft smile, Skylar was more relaxed than I'd ever seen her. "Tell me one thing about you that nobody else knows."

Her nose wrinkled adorably before she blurted, "I've always wanted to go skydiving."

I tilted my head back to look up at the sky, trying to picture her jumping out of a plane and failing. "I'm not sure what I was expecting, but it definitely wasn't that."

"Maybe someday I'll even do it." There was a far-off look in her pretty blue eyes. "But not until Simon is older since it's so dangerous."

I wasn't surprised that she'd put off something she wanted because of the potential negative impact on her son. "You're a great mom."

"Simon makes it easy. He's a great kid."

She had a tendency to minimize compliments, as

though she didn't know what an incredible woman she was. I hoped I'd be able to get her to see herself the way I did at some point. But for now, she'd given me the perfect opening to ask about her son. Her entire face lit up whenever she mentioned him. "What's Simon like?"

"Simon is the typical almost sixteen-year-old boy." She laughed and shook her head. "He's obsessed with baseball, thinks school is boring except for the girls, and can barely wait to get his license so he'll finally be free from me chauffeuring him around."

"Is everything good with his dad's SUV?"

"Yeah, he's been cleaning it inside and out. Steven had taken good care of the vehicle when it had been his, but the fire marshal who took his place wasn't as much of a neat freak." Her nose wrinkled. "Simon has vacuumed the carpet and seats at least four times already and hung an air freshener from the rearview mirror, but the interior still smells like there used to be a deep fryer in the back seat."

In all of the time we had spent together, Skylar had only mentioned Simon's dad a couple of times before quickly moving on to another subject. With what Dean had told me about her lack of a dating life since he died, I assumed it was because he was a painful subject for her to discuss. But if we were going to be in a relationship, I had to get her to open up about him at some point. Now seemed as good a time as any to try. "I've seen your desk at Leaves & Pages. As on top of everything as you are, you're definitely not a neat freak. Did you and Steven bump heads a lot about keeping things organized?"

"Crap." Her gaze slid away from mine, and she bit her bottom lip.

"We don't have to talk about him right now if you're not ready yet."

I was mentally kicking myself for ruining our date when she mumbled, "No...um...I just realized that it isn't fair of me to let you go on thinking I haven't been on a date since Steven died because I've been mourning him all this time. That's not why."

My palms were sweaty, so I swiped my hand against my jeans before reaching out to interlace our fingers. "You can tell me anything."

When she lifted her head, the pain in her eyes was visceral. "I was already reeling from Steven's death when I learned that some things do stay hidden in Mooreville. When I first found out, I was worried that I'd been the last to know. But Sarah promised me that there wasn't any gossip about my marriage. She's the only person I've talked to about what I discovered because I never want it to get out."

I squeezed her hand, hating that she was hurting but grateful that she was finally opening up to me. "Your secrets will always be safe with me."

She took a deep breath before her confession came tumbling out. "Steven had left his personal cell phone in the SUV when he took the boat out fishing on the lake that morning. It was in the box of his things the fire chief brought to me about a week after his death. The battery was dead, and I plugged it into the charger out of habit more than anything else. I don't even remember why I decided to scroll through the pictures except that I was missing him something fierce. I never expected to find a photo of him with another woman. There was just that one, but it was more than enough for me to go looking for an explanation. I thought maybe she was someone he'd saved in a fire before he was promoted, and that was why she had stars in her eyes when she looked at him. Until I found the string of texts that left no doubt about who she was. His mistress who lived on the other side of the county."

*Fuck.* Her reluctance to go out with me despite the strength of the attraction between us suddenly made more sense. She hadn't been grieving her lost love...she'd been trying to get over his betrayal.

"Finding out that he'd been cheating on me was devastating. I couldn't understand how the man I married had turned into the man I buried. One who would betray me like that. Never in a million years would I have thought that Steven would cheat on me. And I had to be super careful with who I talked to about everything. No matter what I was feeling at the time, I needed to protect Simon's memories of his father."

Her eyes pleaded with me to understand. "You did the right thing. If you hadn't kept Steven's secret, your son would've been the one who paid the price."

"I knew that a lot of the spark had gone out of our relationship, but I thought that was just because we weren't teenagers anymore. I figured we were turning into an old married couple even though I was only thirty." She sighed, her shoulders slumping. "In hindsight, I came to realize that was who Steven had been all along. He would never have married me if I hadn't gotten pregnant. He wasn't the man or husband I thought he was. But at least he gave me Simon, who's been the reason I breathe since he was born. Even with that, if he hadn't already been dead when I found out he was cheating on me, I would've been tempted to kill him myself."

"I can't blame you for feeling that way." Not only had her anger been justified, but she'd had to keep it bottled up inside.

Her eyes were full of worry as she bit her bottom lip. "My reaction doesn't scare you?"

"Come here." Scooting closer, I wrapped my arms around her and positioned us so she was sprawled on my chest while I was propped up by the pillows she'd been using. "As angry as you were back then, we both know you never would've done anything to Steven. Except maybe yell at him before divorcing him. Then you would have figured out a way to get along with him because that's what would have been best for your son. And his pain matters to you more than your own."

"Yeah," she sniffled. "I guess you're right."

"Get used to it, baby," I teased in an attempt to lighten the mood, thrilled when the tension left her body.

Sharing my secret with Baxter felt freeing in a way I'd never expected. It was as though a weight had been lifted from my shoulders, and I was finally able to fully relax. I stared up at the sky, enjoying the peace and quiet almost as much as the feel of his strong body beneath mine. When the alarm I had set on my phone to make sure I didn't lose track of time went off, I groaned. "Darn it."

His arms tightened around me as he asked, "Do you have to go?"

"Only if I want to finish any of the chores I planned to get done before Simon gets home." Which seemed much less necessary than when I'd left my house to head here for our date.

"C'mon, up you go." He nudged me to my feet

before piling the containers into the basket and flipping the lid shut. "I'll bring everything inside after I make sure you get home okay."

"You don't have to follow me home," I protested even though the chivalrous offer warmed my heart.

"I let you talk me into not picking you up because I understood why that might spark gossip, but I'm not ending our date by watching you pull out of my driveway. Let me see you home. Please."

The determined glint in his gray eyes warned me he wouldn't back down easily. "It means that much to you?"

"Yes."

One softly spoken word had me rethinking my stance. I wanted to give him what he was asking for, and now that I'd shared my secret with him, the potential gossip didn't seem as big of a problem as I'd thought. Not when I had a feeling that I'd be ready to talk to Simon about Baxter sooner than I expected.

"Okay."

The smile he beamed at me sent butterflies swirling in my belly, and the soft brush of his lips against mine before he helped me into the car intensified the sensation. We weren't even riding together, but I was acutely aware of him during the drive to my house. It was as though his brief kiss had brought my long-dormant libido roaring back to life.

When he pulled into the driveway behind me and got out of his truck to follow me to the door, my thoughts were still on his kiss. I wanted our date to end with another, which had me opening the door wider when I walked inside.

I bit down on my lower lip as Baxter accepted my silent invitation and followed me into the house. His presence was so overwhelming as he crowded my space after kicking the door shut behind us. It wasn't that I didn't want him to be there with me—it had been my idea, after all. It was more the thought of being intimate with someone again, even if all that happened was that kiss I'd been thinking about all the way here. It had been so long since I'd been touched by a man.

The living room looked well lived in, with pictures of Simon on the walls and a pile of his shoes by the door. Thinking about my son reminded me of his father. I reached up and rubbed my breastbone as if that could somehow ease the ache of his betrayal, but it didn't. It never did.

"I love this room," Baxter rumbled behind me, his body so close to mine that the heat of him seared me through my clothes. "Where did you get these curtains?"

A slight dash of both relief and disappointment shafted through me. He'd been so interested in my design choices for the store. I should've known he'd want to talk about the darn curtains. I turned to answer him, and my mouth opened to respond when he dipped his head low and captured my lips with his. Tingles flowed from the top of my head to the bottom of my feet as his tongue teased the edges of my mouth, demanding entrance.

I opened further, groaning as he swept in, his tongue dancing with mine. I longed to join in, but I felt awkward. It had been so long, and Steven never really kissed me like this. It was always a peck. If I was lucky, his lips would linger on mine for a few moments. Another sign I'd missed about how doomed our marriage had been. But Baxter was different. He devoured me with more gusto than he had with the delicious picnic feast we'd just eaten. He made me feel desired.

When he lifted his head, I blurted out the first thought that popped into my head. "This was only our first date."

"Not by my count." He brushed his lips over mine again, gripping my hips with his hands. "It's more like our twentieth if you count all the times we've had coffee together."

"I thought those cappuccinos you brought me were gifts to brighten my mood?"

"Sorry, baby. That's just what I told you to get you to go with me. We've really been dating this whole time," he teased.

I laughed softly. "Sneaky."

"I had to do something to slip behind those walls of yours."

I was surprised to discover how successful he'd been at his mission. Reaching out my hands, I skimmed his chest, bunching his shirt into my fists. If he cared about wrinkling, he didn't show it. Farther down, I rested my hands about his waist and marveled at the abs I could feel just underneath. For a guy in his late thirties who used to be married to his work, his body was amazing.

Shivers raced down my spine as he slid his fingers in my hair, tugging me even closer to him. "I wanted to do this all during lunch," he breathed against my lips.

"Same, honestly." Except for the part where I was sharing my biggest secret with him.

He looked surprised by my admission. "Why didn't you?"

I stared up at him, my brain whirling at his words. "I mean...we were eating. Outside. I couldn't start something with you where someone might see us."

"No? I wouldn't have minded if you did." His lips curved into a wide grin as he leaned in again.

"Was that why the picnic blanket was so big?" I teased, pushing him back. "So we could get hot and heavy if the mood struck?"

"The mood has definitely struck."

His strong arms circled my waist, pulling me into him. Instead of swooping down like last time, he slowed his approach, skimming his lips over mine, teasing me, tantalizing me. I reached up, sliding my hands up his back to grip him as well. His scent surrounded me, the hot smell of man and aftershave. He made me think of decadent nights by the fire. Sex outside in the cool, crisp air of the morning...if only I was daring enough.

Baxter groaned once more against my lips before shifting down to slide his hands under my knees. Startled, I pushed him back, my heart racing with the thought of what he was about to do. Like an idiot, I asked anyway. "What are you doing?"

"Picking you up so we can continue this else-where? Or am I misreading the signals?" He pulled back, his brows drawn down into a frown. "I don't want to rush you into anything, even if it's technically our twentieth date."

My cheeks heated with a mixture of desire and embarrassment. "You're not rushing me. I want more kisses. It's just...you were trying to pick me up."

His brows drew together. "And?"

"And? I mean. I'm not the lightest woman in the world. You'll either drop me or hurt your back." I hated admitting the fact that being picked up not only frightened me but further showcased our differences. I was a curvy woman with a teenage son, where Baxter was a billionaire bachelor with lean muscles and a body that could've made him millions if he needed them. As strong as he was, the fact that he thought he could easily carry me somewhere was laughable. No one had picked me up since I was a kid.

His face darkened for a moment as he stared at me, his gray eyes drifting up and down my body. A sharp nod of his head was the only warning I got before he bent over and scooped me over his shoulder. Within moments, I was facedown, my gaze glued to his fabulous ass as he strode into the living room.

What was amazing was that he didn't seem bothered by my size or the fact that I wasn't in the same toned league as him. He'd probably dated models half my size when he lived in New York, but he seemed completely content maneuvering me. I was never maneuvered. Not by anyone. Yet I found it oddly thrilling that he was able to put me where he wanted me.

"I get that you're not used to compliments, but never diminish yourself in front of me. If I didn't think I could handle you, I wouldn't have done it. Trust me. I'm more than able to handle you. I've waited months to get you right where I want you. The last thing I'm going to do is fuck this up now."

After setting me on the couch, he dropped onto the cushion next to me and motioned for me to sit on his lap. I wasn't sure if he was trying to prove a point or just be flirtatious, but I sure as heck didn't want to upset him any more than I had. He just didn't understand. Men who looked like him never had to worry about the same things I did. Not that I'd been overly concerned about how I looked until I met Baxter. Being attractive to men hadn't been important before he came into my life.

His hands patted his thigh as he waited for me, his quick smile once more meeting his eyes. Shaking my head, I stood, prepared to sit on his lap when his fingers dug into my hips. "Look at me."

I turned, my gaze meeting his. From there, he turned me the rest of the way until I stood between his thighs. Lowering his hands, he coaxed one leg then the other until I was straddling him, my lips hovering above his. He threaded his hands back in my hair and pulled me down for a soul-searing kiss. Groaning, my hips rocked against Baxter, arousal gathering lower. I hadn't felt this needy in so long.

With fierce desire coursing through my veins, it didn't matter what I looked like. It didn't matter what the house looked like or the chores I'd planned on doing. It didn't matter that my son was coming home from school soon. All that mattered was the sexy man underneath me, arching his hips to meet mine. Baxter's hands slid around my waist to grip my ass, a groan tearing through his throat as he palmed them.

"Let me devour you. Give me a dessert better than those chocolate truffles, beautiful," he whispered against my lips, and all I could do was nod.

In a flash, he lifted me off his lap and set me on the couch. His fingers fiddled with the button and zipper on my jeans, but soon those too were gone, leaving me in just a shirt and my lacy panties. I squeezed my thighs together, but he would have none of that. With gentle but insistent movements, he spread my legs apart, glancing up at me before licking his lips.

I was drenched, so much so that I was sure my panties were soaked. His thumbs skimmed the lace edges before dipping just under the fabric to graze the sensitive skin of my pussy lips. Groaning, I leaned back on the couch and let my legs fall farther apart. Baxter bent low, sliding his cheek across my inner thigh before blazing a trail of hot kisses up to my clit, his tongue gliding over the wet fabric as he lapped at the sensitive nub.

Reaching down, I gripped his hair, drawing him even closer. His hot chuckle seared my skin as he continued to tease me through the lace. Before I could beg him to do more, he hooked his thumbs around the band and slid them off, laying them on top of my jeans. I glanced over at the clock, not wanting to be distracted but also not wanting my son to walk in on me in flagrante delicto. It would be beyond mortifying.

His mouth was back on me, kissing, licking, nibbling, driving all rational thought from my mind. He slid his hands under my hips, pulling my legs over his shoulders, arching me off the couch. When Baxter licked my pussy, it was as if I was the best tasting dessert in the world. He moaned. He sighed. He groaned. Pleasure coiled through my body as he tipped his head lower and speared me with his tongue.

Baxter licked deep, filling me as best he could, flattening out his tongue to give me as much sensation as possible. I had never felt anything like this. Never been devoured with this much enthusiasm, as though Baxter couldn't get enough.

He kept licking me, tasting me. He ate me out like I was his last meal. His attention alone set my stomach to fluttering, much less what he was doing with his heavenly lips. Pulling back, he stared at me through my splayed thighs, holding my gaze as he slid a finger inside me.

Unable to keep quiet, I tipped my head back and moaned, my core fluttering around his digit. Lord almighty. If just his finger felt this good, what would his dick feel like? My muscles squeezed at the thought of him filling me up, stuffing me full while he stared at me with that erotic, intense gaze.

Baxter pumped his finger in and out a few times, stretching me just a little bit before sliding out to ease two fingers into me. It felt better than I could have ever hoped for. The stretch was intense as his fingertips sparked along all my nerve endings until I was a writhing, quivering mess.

I looked back down, shuddering at his knowing, seductive smirk. I wanted to look away, but I couldn't. He held me there with his gaze, and I watched as his fingers slid in and out of me, the sight sexier than anything I'd ever seen before. He winked and dipped his head back down to lick at my clit. Lightning shot through my body as he found just the right spot and kept at it, not moving, not varying pressure, just listening to my body and going from there.

My body stiffened as my stomach plummeted. It was as though I was free-falling even though I was safely on the couch. I tensed as pleasure flooded my body, crying out as the orgasm hit me hard and didn't let go. Neither did Baxter. He kept pumping his fingers, riding out my orgasm until I was a babbling mess.

Once my body settled, he stayed kneeling between my knees, smiling at my pussy as if the mere act of getting me off gave him pleasure as well. Smiling, I let him drop my feet to the floor and gave it a second before sitting back up to face him. I leaned in, brushing my lips against his and tasting myself. It sent another ripple of desire through me.

I reached down, my lips widening even farther. We still had time before Simon got home. As I reached for his belt, his hand encircled my wrist. "Sorry, beautiful. I'll have to take a rain check."

All the good feelings I had experienced evaporated in an instant, doubt quickly creeping in. He must have been able to tell because his hands slid up to cradle my face, a tender smile on his lips. "It's not because I don't want to. Trust me, I want you more than anything." He took my hand and brought it to the front of his pants. The bulge behind the zipper was unreal and eased my bruised pride. "I just don't ever want things rushed between us. When I finally get my cock inside your perfect pussy, I'm going to take my time. And you're going to be damn sure you're ready to be mine."

I t had only taken one taste for me to become addicted to Skylar. Keeping myself in check after giving her an orgasm had been one of the most difficult things I'd ever done. I'd wanted nothing more than to sink my cock into her pussy and pound away until we came together. It had taken all of my willpower to walk out of her house and drive back home.

I'd been worried she would try to pull back after what had happened between us on her couch, but she'd seemed more open than usual when I called her last night. We'd talked for about an hour before she had to go, and the conversation had gone a long way toward easing my concern. But I was still anxious to see her today. To make sure those gorgeous blue eyes of hers didn't hold any regret. To confirm I wasn't moving too fast for her.

That was why I'd gotten up earlier than usual and headed into my office. I wanted to be here when Skylar came to the store, and she'd told me that she was coming in today as soon as Simon left for school.

When I heard footsteps sooner than expected, I realized my first visitor of the day wasn't the one I'd been hoping for. At least Dean was carrying two to-go cups of coffee when he walked into my office. After handing me one, he rolled the executive chair —that had been replaced by the one from her store that Skylar insisted I have—from the corner of the room to the side of my desk and dropped onto it. "How did your date go?"

"It was good."

Dean leaned forward, tilting his head to the side. "It was good? That's all you have to say after how long it took you to get her to say yes?"

I should've known he'd want more details. Scraping my hands through my hair, I sighed. "It was better than good."

"Damn, I thought I'd get more information from you than that since I've been your wingman with her."

I wasn't accustomed to feeling so content, but

even though things had gone much better than I'd expected with Skylar yesterday, I wasn't past all of the potential hurdles. There was a lightness in my chest as I took a deep breath, considering how much I wanted to share with him. "I'm not going to kiss and tell."

He beamed a big grin at me. "So there was kissing."

I took a sip of my coffee to hide my satisfied smirk, but the knowing gleam in his eyes made it clear that he caught on to what I was trying to do. "Like I said, our date was better than good."

"I'm really happy for you, man." He swiveled the chair back and forth. "Where'd you take her?"

"We had a picnic at my house."

His brows drew together. "Huh. I figured you'd put all your money to good use and woo your woman properly. Take her somewhere fancy to impress her."

Skylar wasn't the kind of woman who needed fancy to be impressed. She just wanted me to show her that she mattered to me. Her disinterest in my bank account and what I could provide her with just made me want to give her more. "You know how nosy everyone can be. Skylar thought it was too soon to make tongues wag since it was only our official first date."

He pursed his lips and nodded. "I can see why she'd want to keep things quiet for now. She has a kid to worry about, and I had at least a dozen people ask me about that lunch you two had at Trattoria when she signed her lease. With her not dating in so long and you being who you are, there was a lot of speculation."

"I understand her reasons." I heaved a deep sigh. "But I'm not sure how I feel about keeping our relationship private."

His eyes widened while he grinned. "You're pulling out the R-word after only one date?"

I slipped my hands into my pockets and leaned back in my chair. "As far as I'm concerned, we've been together since the day she signed the lease and we had lunch together at Trattoria."

Dean rubbed the back of his neck before nodding. "I guess I can see why you'd feel that way. Neither of you has been dating anyone else, and even though the picnic was your first official date, you've been spending a lot of time together under the guise of helping her with her business."

"It wasn't all a pretense. I actually did help her." My mouth was dry as I admitted, "I already feel as though I know her better than any other woman I've dated. If I had my way, I'd put a full-page ad in the newspaper announcing she was mine."

He laughed, shaking his head. "That's just your inner caveman talking."

"Never had one of those before." Something about warning off other guys from Skylar appealed to me on a deep level. She had no idea how damn gorgeous she was and didn't notice the attention she garnered from other guys. Although we were in the early stages of our relationship and I didn't have the right, I wanted to warn off any guy who might think about asking her out.

"If you do something like that, you'll definitely scare her off. Then you'd lose all of the progress you've made with her by doing something sure to piss her off."

My jaw ached from how hard I was clenching my teeth. "I didn't say I was actually going to do it, just that I wanted to. I don't like that we have to keep what's happening between us a secret."

"Are you worried her hesitation is because she's not over Steven?"

I had waded into dangerous conversation waters. Skylar's secret wasn't mine to share. "No, we talked about it, and she was very clear that she wants to know where this is going before she talks to Simon about us. Since she hasn't dated anyone else before me, she isn't sure how he's going to react."

"Good."

Almost as though we'd conjured her up by talking about her, Skylar walked into my office and came to an abrupt stop when she spotted Dean sitting across from me. "Sorry, I didn't mean to interrupt."

My cousin whirled his chair around to smile at her. "No need to apologize. I was just grilling Baxter about your date."

"Oh." Skylar's eyes were worried as she approached us.

"You don't need to worry about Dean. He isn't going to gossip about us with anyone." I shot him a warning look. "Not even his brothers."

"My lips are sealed," Dean promised.

The concern in her gorgeous blue eyes was obvious, but I was the only one who knew the true reason behind it. "Not that he even has a lot to say. All he knows is that you finally stopped resisting my charm."

Dean set his coffee down on my desk and pressed his hands together as though he was praying. "Maybe you'll take pity on me and share how the date went since this guy isn't sharing any of the good stuff. You'd think he'd be a little more forthcoming since I've been his wingman with you."

The tension left Skylar's curvy body as she quirked a brow. "His wingman, huh? So he didn't just happen to show up when you were showing me the space downstairs?"

"Oops." Dean shot out of his seat and grabbed his cup. "Sorry, gotta run. I have a...meeting I can't miss."

Skylar's eyes widened at his abrupt departure. "I hope he knows I'm not really going to hold his wingman antics against him. It's just fun to tease."

"He'll be fine," I assured her. "Worry about me instead. I missed you."

The guard she'd had up while my cousin was around dropped, and the desire in her gorgeous blue eyes was impossible to miss. "I missed you, too."

"Come here." I crooked my finger, and my lips curved into a satisfied smirk when she didn't hesitate to circle my desk to stand directly in front of me. Getting to my feet, I dipped my head to claim her mouth in a deep kiss. It felt damn good to be able to act on the urge after keeping my hands off her for so long.

Her eyes were hazy with passion when I finally lifted my head again. "Thank you for the flowers."

I'd left a bouquet of pink roses on her desk this morning. I would have had them delivered to her house instead, but that wouldn't have been honoring her request to keep things between us private. The florist would have spread that news high and low. But I wanted to do something to honor the step she'd taken with me yesterday—both with how she'd opened up about her marriage and letting me get a taste of her pussy. So I drove one town over to buy the flowers and delivered them to Leaves & Pages when nobody else was around. If anyone asked her about the roses, I figured she could just say she bought them for the store since they went well with the design. "You're welcome. I wanted to make sure you knew I was thinking about you."

"You definitely succeeded." Stroking her palms up my chest, she fiddled with the collar of my dress shirt. "I actually wanted to let you know that Simon's grandparents called this morning before I took him to school. They were hoping he could spend the day with them tomorrow, and he was on board with the plan. So I suddenly find myself with some unexpected free time on my hands and am wondering if maybe you want to do something."

I felt a rush of adrenaline at her news. "Hell yes,

I want to do something with you. How much time can you give me?"

"As much as you want. I don't need to be home until after dinner. They won't drop him back off until around eight or nine."

Dean's comment about pulling out all the stops to impress Skylar popped into my head, and an idea formed as I recalled something she'd shared with me during our picnic. She wouldn't care about the money I was going to spend to make our date happen, but she would appreciate the thought I put into it. I was going to woo the fuck out of her tomorrow.

W hen Baxter had asked me to meet him at his house for our second date, I'd had the strangest urge to march him down Main Street, where everyone would see us. My reaction had brought home the point he'd made about the time we'd spent together over the past couple of months. We knew each other much better than most people did this early in a relationship. And it was scary to admit, but I'd been falling for him a little bit at a time without realizing it was happening until now. Our non-dating had accomplished more than most people's dating did.

Pulling up in front of his house, I found Baxter waiting on the front porch for me again. This time, though, other people were milling about the property. A gardener was trimming the hedges on the far side of the house, and the man who answered the door when I came to apologize was on the porch talking to Baxter. Or at least he was trying to—all of Baxter's attention was on me, so he wasn't paying much attention to whatever was being said.

The man remained where he was while Baxter came toward the car to open my door for me. I loved how chivalrous he always was with me. "Thanks."

"My pleasure, beautiful." With his hand on my lower back, he guided me up the steps. "Skylar, this is Peter. He's the one who keeps my life running on a day-to-day basis."

I smiled at Peter. "Hello."

"Nice to see you again, ma'am."

My cheeks heated as I remembered how I'd tried to get him to take the chocolate sheet cake when I'd nearly chickened out on apologizing to Baxter. "Please, call me Skylar."

His gaze slid toward Baxter before he nodded and held a tablet out to me. "If you could check the box and sign your name, everything will be set for your date when you arrive."

"What am I signing?" I asked, peering down at the fine print listed.

Baxter covered the top of the screen. "Nuh-uh. That would ruin the surprise."

"As my business consultant, shouldn't you be advising me against signing anything I haven't read first?" I muttered as I tapped my finger to check the box and then drew my name on the screen.

"Normally, yes," he conceded with a grin. Taking the tablet from me, he handed it back to Peter, who headed inside, leaving the door open for us. "But you can trust me. I'll always have your best interests at heart."

"Where are you taking me?" I asked as he led me through the house.

When we stepped through the French doors off the kitchen, he answered, "Remember when I asked you to tell me something nobody else knows about you?"

My gaze darted toward where we had our picnic on the lawn just two days ago. "Of course, I remember. It was our first date."

"Twentieth," he corrected with a grin.

"Agree to disagree."

"Uh-huh." He pointed to the left. "I thought you might like to make that dream come true."

When I saw the helicopter, I gasped. "Did you forget the part where I said skydiving was going to have to stay on my bucket list at least until Simon started college? There's no way I'm going to jump out of that."

"I didn't forget a thing. Helo jumps aren't for beginners." He laughed as he tugged me outside.

My brow wrinkled in confusion. "How do you know so much about skydiving? You didn't mention that you'd gone before when we talked about it."

"I haven't, but I did some research into it."

His answer made me smile. "I should have known."

His thumb brushed over my knuckles. "Whatever it takes to make your dreams come true."

Butterflies swarmed in my belly, and they had nothing to do with my nerves over the helicopter waiting for us. "If we're not jumping out of that thing, what are we doing?"

"I'm taking you to an indoor skydiving place in Indianapolis. You'll get the rush of skydiving without having to jump out of a plane."

That sounded amazing, but I didn't understand why we weren't driving there. It only took two hours to drive to Indy. "And you rented a helicopter to get us there?"

"No, baby. I own the helicopter."

My eyes widened at the reminder of his wealth,

and I was still wrapping my head around the fact that he owned the helicopter as he helped me inside.

"I've never flown in a helicopter before," I whispered as he buckled the harness for me.

As he kissed his way along my jawline, his breath was hot in my ear when he replied, "I'm glad I get to experience this first with you."

I was trembling in anticipation when he climbed into his seat and let the pilot know we were ready to go. He held my hand during the fifty minutes it took us to get to Indianapolis while I pointed out all the sights along the way. A car was waiting for us when we arrived, and the indoor skydiving place was a quick drive from the heliport that I'd had no idea was downtown.

We were greeted by an indoor skydiving flight instructor when we arrived, who took us on a quick tour of the facility. I was in awe of the glass tunnel where we were going to dive. It was about fifteen feet wide and five stories high.

"This is your first time with us, right?" After Baxter and I nodded, Brian tapped the screen of the tablet he was holding. "And it looks as though you've already filled out the necessary waivers, so all that's left to do before you go into orientation is put on your jumpsuits."

After pulling the jumpsuit over my clothes and braiding my hair, I grinned at Baxter. "If I'd known this was what we were doing, I wouldn't have worried about what I wore on our date today."

"You always look gorgeous to me, no matter what you wear."

"Flatterer," I mumbled, my cheeks filling with heat over the compliment.

"I'm only telling the truth."

There was no mistaking the sincerity shining from his gray eyes. Or the slight bulge in his jump-suit that confirmed his desire for me. "Ah-hum, you look great too."

He swept his hand down the length of his body. "I can't help my reaction to you, beautiful. You make me feel like I'm a teenager again."

As Brian came back into the room, I whispered, "Maybe the fear of injury will help."

"We'll spend about ten minutes going over what to expect when you're in the wind tunnel, including the hand signals we'll use and practicing the flight position." He pointed toward a door off to the left. "Your first jump will be instructor-assisted, so we adjust your body positioning as needed."

Baxter slung his arm around my shoulders,

pulling me against his side. "Who's going in with Skylar?"

Brian's gaze darted between us, taking in Baxter's territorial stance. "Um, I could ask Heather to do it?"

"Heather sounds perfect."

I couldn't stop my giggle at Baxter's response. He didn't know a single thing about the other instructor except that she was female, but that was enough for him. "Okay, please watch this video while I go get her."

Brian pressed play on an instructional video before leaving the room. Only half paying attention to what was happening on the screen, I murmured, "Should I make sure Heather isn't helping you during your first flight?"

"No worries there, beautiful. I'll make sure Brian goes into the tunnel with me."

It was hard to be angry with him for being territorial when he applied the same standard to himself. And when Heather turned out to be a pretty brunette in her twenties, I was relieved that she was my instructor and not his.

Brian and Heather stayed off to the side until the video was done, and then they had us practice our positioning. Belly down on the bench with my back arched, my chin up, and my arms and legs stretched out to mimic the position I needed to use when I got into the wind tunnel, I felt ridiculous. When I caught Baxter staring at me, I rolled my eyes. "I bet I don't look gorgeous now."

"That'd be a wager you'd lose." His gaze drifted down the length of my body. "You'd still be beautiful walking around in a potato sack."

Heather sighed in appreciation. Once our training was done and she walked with me into the tunnel, she said, "Nice job. Your boyfriend is so sweet."

"He really is," I agreed with a smile. "He planned this whole date for me because I mentioned I wanted to go skydiving sometime."

"This is a great way to start and a heck of a rush," she promised right before the wind started.

Holding my right arm and leg, Heather helped me circle around the tunnel a few times before lifting into the air with me. We rotated in unison, moving up and down several times. She'd been right. Indoor skydiving still gave me a heck of a rush. It was even better when I got to go by myself, with her staying in the tunnel just in case I needed help. And I had just as much fun watching Baxter during his turn.

When we were finished and back in the car to

head to the heliport, I stared down at the flight certificate Heather gave me. "I can't believe you did this. I've never had someone pay attention to me like you do."

He stopped at a red light and lifted my hand to brush a kiss against my knuckles. "I would've taken you to do the real thing, but I know you're not ready yet."

"Two and a half more years to go, and then I can take a few more risks. Simon will be off to college."

"We'll save that for another first." My heart swelled as he casually mentioned doing something so far into the future with me. "But take a chance on me in the meantime."

"I will, Baxter. I really will." Considering how distrustful I'd been when we met, my answer shouldn't have been easy. It slipped out without thought, but I discovered I meant every word. He'd somehow managed to do what I'd thought was impossible—earn my trust.

## 15

Taking the helicopter had been important because the time we saved traveling to and from Indianapolis meant we didn't need to rush during dinner...and whatever might happen after. I wasn't expecting to have sex with Skylar tonight, but I sure as fuck wanted to get another taste of her pussy. I was already addicted to her, and I was driven to get her hooked on the pleasure I could give her.

The look Skylar gave me as she sipped her water was pure seduction. She might not have meant it that way, but that was what it was doing to me. Knowing her, she probably had no clue, but that was part of what was so alluring about her. She was sexy without even trying. I brought the napkin up to my mouth to wipe away my drink before standing up and dropping it onto the table.

Her breath hitched as I stalked toward her, and I made no secret about my intent. Our date had gone better than I'd anticipated, and I'd had high expectations for it. The pure joy on her face when she'd been skydiving in the tunnel had been more than worth the effort it had taken to plan our day together, but it paled compared to how I felt when she said she was ready to take a chance on me.

We'd been circling around each other for far too long. My balls drew up even more as I looked down at the table, a coy smile tilting the side of her lips. From the moment I saw her, I wanted her in my bed, and now, it was finally going to happen. I reached out my hand, trying to be a gentleman—even though I wanted to throw her over my shoulder again—and smiled when she took it.

It took every ounce of restraint not to just toss her up on the table and have my way with her. Instead, I took her to my bedroom and shut the door, allowing her a moment to take the space in. The massive bed in the middle looked empty—too empty. Stepping up behind Skyler, I grasped the tab of the zipper on the back of her dress and slowly pulled down, giving her ample time to say no if she wanted.

I would have respected that, but my cock desperately wanted to be deep inside her. I hoped she wouldn't say no. The zipper made a loud buzz in the silent room, the hiss only punctuated by our rapid breathing. With each expanse of skin revealed, I slid my lips across the soft surface.

The perfume she wore filled my lungs, making my brain buzz. Once she was fully unzipped, I slid my hands up to the top and began pulling down—again, giving her ample time to ask me to slow down if she needed to. Her dress was a puddle on the floor, leaving her in a pair of pink lace panties and a matching bra.

Skylar turned to me, her lips parted, and looked me up and down. "It's not fair that I'm the only one getting undressed."

Smirking, I dragged her close, pecking the top of her pert nose. "Fair, probably not, but I promise I'll make it worth it to you." What I didn't want to tell her was my clothes were the only thing keeping me from just ravaging her. I wanted to make tonight special and not jump on her like a teenager with no control. My clothes helped me keep just one more layer of civility between us.

She chuckled and dropped to the floor, completely derailing my brain. There was no way I'd last more than a minute if she took me in her mouth now, and I'd be damned if I was the one to come first. Not going to happen.

Ignoring her adorable pout as I stood her up, I slid my hands around Skylar's waist and turned her again so that her back was firmly against the side wall. From there, her underwear just had to go. It was an impediment I could no longer abide. With slow, agonizing movements, I inched the scraps of lace down, forcing my erection to behave itself. I would have my moment soon, but not until after I had Skylar screaming my name.

Once her panties were off, I could see that she was glistening with arousal for me. I couldn't wait any longer for another taste of her, so I lifted one of her legs and went to work, sliding my tongue up one side of her lips and down the other.

She moaned and thumped her head back against the wall—music to my ears, but it still wasn't enough. Flattening my tongue, I started at her entrance and swiped my way up, circling her clit for a moment before going back down to do it all over again. Over and over, I licked her just like my favorite ice cream, savoring every taste, every feel, every inch of her.

Soon, she was writhing at every touch, thrusting

her hips against me as if she couldn't get enough. Now we were getting somewhere.

I gripped her hips, holding her in place as I licked inside her, letting her taste explode on my tongue. Pulling back, I slid two fingers into her, not even bothering with just one. She was so wet. And so ready for me. With a grin, I shoved up, filling her to the hilt. She groaned and rocked back and forth on my thick digits, her hips swiveling as she found her pleasure.

Her clit was so hard and needy as I went back to it, my tongue circling the nub. Soft whimpers spilled out of her mouth, but she was still being quiet for some reason. I had no clue why. It was just her and me right now since I'd given the staff the night off. "Scream for me, beautiful. Let me hear how good this feels." I was sure having to live at home with her son, she had to keep herself quiet, but in the sanctuary of my house, anything went.

Her moans got a bit louder, and I didn't try to get her to do more than that. I knew it was probably hard enough for her to fully let go as it was. Soon, she bucked against me, her hips humping my fingers as the orgasm took over. "Bax!" she cried out, her body clenching around my fingers. Her grip was so tight around me, my eyes rolled back in my head. I couldn't wait to feel those muscles grip my cock. And I wanted to hear that shortened version of my name spill from her lips when she came with my cock buried deep inside her pussy.

"That's it, beautiful. Let go for me." Her body shuddered as aftershocks ran through her. Pulling out, I ignored her whimpers of protest as I gathered her in my arms and carried her to the bed. One of these days, she was going to get used to it.

She sprawled out over my sheets, her chest heaving as she took in deep breaths. She was a vision, glistening with sweat and her body languid as she lay there. Standing over her, I made a show of unbuttoning my sleeves and rolling them up to reveal my muscled forearms. She knew the strength and power of my hands, but now she got to feast her eyes on me.

Skylar's eyes widened as she watched my slow striptease. Each button took nearly a minute to undo as I dragged things out to further entice her. She probably had no clue how those innocent blushes and small smiles went straight to my cock. My rock-hard shaft pulsed against my pants, desperate to be free.

She pulled her bottom lip into her mouth and bit down on it, nearly driving my need to take things slow out the window. A soft growl escaped my lips as

I tugged the shirttails out of my pants and tossed the whole thing to the floor. Next were my pants and boxer briefs, but at this point, I didn't have any further patience to continue dragging things out. I needed her. I needed her just as badly as I needed air. Reaching over to the drawer, I pulled out an unopened box of condoms and began fiddling with the plastic wrapper.

She looked at me, her head tilted as if trying to figure out what I was doing. "I wanted to make things special tonight. I didn't want to assume, but I wanted to be prepared just in case. I grabbed these when I bought your flowers, a town over so nobody would be talking about it and put two plus two together to come up with you and me having sex. If I haven't made it that obvious, I haven't had a woman share my bed in years."

The smile on her face lit up the entire room. She beamed at me as if I were a superhero to her. And that hurt worst of all, knowing that something as simple as taking the time to care for her meant so much. It put into light just how badly she had been treated in the past. If anything, it was going to be my new mission to make sure I took every bad memory she had and erased it, putting new ones in its place.

The plastic gave way, and I tore open the box,

pulling out one of the condoms inside. Grabbing the edge of the foil with my teeth, I ripped the packet, removing the condom. I went to place it over my cock, when Skylar's hands reached out to stop me.

"Please, let me."

I couldn't say no. Placing my hands at the back of my head, I stared down as she forced the ring over the head of my cock and rolled the latex down over my shaft. Who knew condoms could be so sexy? Once I was fully sheathed, I laid her back down on the bed and loomed over her. She reached out her hand to slide it across my cheek, and I nuzzled into her palm, reveling in her touch.

Since she'd already had one orgasm, I didn't feel bad about finally taking my pleasure. Lining up my head with her entrance, I slid in, groaning as her snug heat enveloped me, surrounding me with sensation. Her gasp intermingled with my groan as I leaned over and rocked my pelvis forward, fully seating myself deep within her. "Holy fuck, you feel so damn good."

I gripped her hips, bringing her legs to wrap around my back. Reaching down, I slid my hands behind her back to undo her bra and pull it off her. That, too, ended up on the floor along with my other clothes. Her breasts were more than a handful, the pebbled tips begging for my mouth. "So fucking beautiful."

Bending low, I sucked one of her nipples into my mouth, flicking my tongue against the peak. "Oh, Bax," she breathed, writhing beneath me.

I shifted to the other side, nipping at the rounded swell before giving that nipple the same attention. When I lifted my head again, her lips looked plump and flushed. And enticing. Bending low, I slid my mouth against hers, sighing at the delicate softness as I worked my dick in and out of her wetness.

Fingers digging into her hips, I pulled out, swallowing her moan. I broke the kiss off and looked down to where our bodies joined. It was such an erotic sight. There was no way I would last as long as I wanted to. Not with her body coaxing out such delicious shivers from mine. I slammed back in, grinning at her grunt of pleasure.

"Knew it was going to be good, but I could never have dreamed being inside you would feel like coming home."

My balls tightened, tingling, drawing up until I was unable to even think straight. Pulling her legs away from me, I bent them forward, changing the angle up. From there, I drove into her, aiming for the spot that would drive her the most wild. Her head thrashed back and forth as our bodies collided. Reaching down, I ran my thumb over her clit, hoping to make her come one more time. "Give me another, beautiful. I want to hear you cry out for me again."

I looked away, forcing my brain to think about anything but the tingles forming at the base of my spine, but it was no use. My cock swelled as I slammed home one last time, come spurting from me. She didn't have her second orgasm yet, but I wasn't going to let that deter me. I rocked against her again, riding that wave of pleasure as I kept working her over.

Though I was softening, I stayed inside, shivering as her muscles clamped down, milking me as her orgasm barreled through her. This time, her "Bax" was much louder, ringing off the walls. My grin was bigger than before as I rolled away from her body after she came down from the pleasure. Gripping the base of the condom, I pulled out and kissed Skylar's forehead.

"You just lay right there. I'll be right back."

The bright lights of the bathroom sent spots dancing in front of my eyes as I made my way over to the sink. I disposed of the condom as quickly as I could and cleaned up before grabbing a separate washcloth and holding it under the warm water. She was already squirming as I made my way over but stilled as I cleaned her up.

Her smile was soft and warm as I dragged the cloth over her pussy. The small giggle as I found a particularly ticklish area was beyond adorable. Once she was cleaned, I tossed the rag over in the vicinity of the bathroom, not really giving a damn where it fell. Grinning, I crawled back onto the bed and pulled her into my arms.

"I really have to go at some point," she teased, pushing against me with mock ferocity.

"I know, but I get to keep you for a little while yet. Simon won't be home again for another two or three hours." I wished I had more time with her tonight, but I wasn't going to complain after what had just happened between us. Even though I was looking forward to the day when I got to wake up with her in my arms, I'd take what she could give me until then.

Instead of focusing on the marketing materials I was trying to finish, I was mooning over the gorgeous roses Baxter had given me when the man himself pulled me from my thoughts. "You seem nervous."

Glancing up, I spotted him standing in the back doorway with another bouquet of roses clutched in his large hands. I had left the door cracked open in the hope that he'd venture down to see me at some point today. It was amazing what a difference a few days—along with a romantic picnic, helicopter ride, indoor skydiving, and a few mind-blowing orgasms—could make. I'd gone from trying to avoid him as much as possible to missing him in the blink of an eye. Which was why I'd added an important task to my to-do list today. "That's because I am nervous."

"How come?" he asked, his brows drawing together as he strode toward me.

"Simon is getting dropped off downtown today so he can help me out with some stuff here. I thought it would be a good idea to get him used to the space before the grand opening since he's going to work with me over the summer."

Baxter checked his watch. "He'll be here in about twenty minutes?"

"Yeah." I beamed a smile at him, pleased that he'd paid attention to my son's schedule during the time we'd spent working together on the shop's build-out.

"I'll make myself scarce before he shows up." He set the roses down on my desk. They were the same pale pink as the last bouquet and in a matching vase that fit in perfectly with the vibe of Leaves & Pages. "If you put these out front, maybe he won't wonder what's up with all the flowers."

With what I was planning to do today, Simon noticing them wouldn't be a bad thing. "I can't remember the last time I got flowers, and now I have two vases full of gorgeous roses in just a few days. Are you going to give me flowers after every date?"

"Maybe not every time since I plan on taking up most of your free time, but you can plan on lots of roses in your future." He circled my desk to stroke his thumb across my cheek. "I like seeing that look in your eyes when I give them to you."

His answer was exactly what I'd come to expect from Baxter...and perfect. "I'm looking forward to spending most of my free time with you even more than the flowers you'll give me in the future."

"You can't be so sweet, beautiful. It makes me want to do this." His mouth crashed down on mine for a quick, hard kiss. It was just long enough that my wits were scattered when he lifted his head and asked, "Is there anything I can help you with until Simon gets here?"

My answering nod was hesitant. "Actually, there is something that only you can help me with."

He glanced over his shoulder at the door as he trailed his fingers down my arm. "Do you need to relieve some tension, beautiful?"

"What? No, not that," I sputtered, shaking my head even while goose bumps spread across my skin in the wake of his touch. "After the amazing day we spent together yesterday, I've been thinking that I should talk to Simon about us sooner rather than later."

His head jerked back, his eyes going wide. "You want me here when you talk to him?"

I shook my head. "No, I just need you to reassure me that it's the right thing to do. You're positive that this isn't just a fling that will end now that I've slept with you? Because if that's all this is, then I don't want to say anything to him."

He cupped my cheeks with his palms and brushed his lips over mine. "Is there something I've done to give you that impression?"

"No." I heaved a deep sigh before burying my face in his chest as I mumbled, "I'm just freaking out a little over here."

He stroked my back. "If it helps, I can say with the utmost certainty that my interest in you will not disappear just because we had sex."

"It's not just the chase?" I voiced my deepest fear.

"I already caught you, beautiful." He pressed my palm against his hard-on. "And it only made me want you even more."

I heaved a deep sigh of relief. "Okay, good. Then I guess I'll be telling my son about us today."

The smile he beamed at me was worth all my nerves. "Does that mean I can take you out on a real date soon?"

"Hey now, you've already given me the two most romantic dates of my life." I swatted his chest playfully, but his expression remained determined. "But yes, you can take me out somewhere all the prying eyes in Mooreville will see us. Just as soon as I know Simon is okay with me dating."

"That is fucking fantastic news, beautiful." He brushed his mouth against mine again. "I can't wait to take you out for dinner. Dancing too, if you want to go."

"Yes, please. I'd love to." I couldn't remember the last time I'd gone dancing. Not counting my wedding, it might've been when I was still in high school.

"Let me know how your talk goes with Simon, and I'll make the plans for our next date."

"Friday night." At his look of confusion, I added, "Simon is supposed to sleep over at a friend's house. If you want to go out dancing after dinner, Friday night would work great because I won't need to worry about when I get home."

His eyes turned heated. "I want you all night. We can wake up early if Simon and his friend won't sleep in. But I want you in my bed as late as you can stay. My chef can make you whatever you want for breakfast."

I pressed the pad of my index finger against his lips. "You had me at 'I want you all night.' You don't have to bribe me with a fancy breakfast, although I'll still take it."

"Are you gonna stay until morning?"

"Yup." I smiled up at him. "I might even get a little tipsy while we're out dancing since I don't need to worry about driving home."

"I didn't think it was possible with how amazing last night was, but you made today even better than yesterday. Thank you."

The things he said to me...it was no wonder I was ready to tell my son about Baxter. "Thank you for somehow making every day better than the last."

"My new mission in my life," he murmured against my lips, claiming them in another passionate kiss before reluctantly pulling away. "I'll be upstairs if you need me, beautiful."

Knowing he wouldn't hesitate to step in and help me with Simon if our conversation went south was exactly what I'd needed to soothe my nerves. Giving him a little nudge, I promised, "Will do, but you better get going so you don't distract me into forgetting Simon is coming. I don't want him to find out about us by walking in on us putting my desk to good use."

He flashed me a sexy grin and patted the top of my desk. "Thanks for the idea."

"Holy crap," I whispered, fanning myself when he walked out.

I'd barely pulled myself together when Simon showed up. His grandpa had taken him out for a highway driving lesson this morning since his road test was coming up soon. "Hey, Mom," he called as the bell over the front door jingled.

"Back here!" Instead of meeting him out front, I waited for him to come into my office. "How did the driving go?"

"Good." His grin was huge. "I got Grandpa's car all the way up to seventy."

The thought of my baby boy driving that fast terrified me, which was why he'd wanted to go out with his grandfather instead. He stayed a lot calmer than I did when Simon was behind the wheel. "I'm glad it went well."

He dropped onto the chair on the other side of my desk. "What's the plan for today? Is there stuff you want me to help with here today? I have some homework I need to get done tonight."

"I don't have much of a plan for today, but there was something I wanted to talk to you about." I took a deep breath, attempting to soothe my nerves. "We don't have secrets between you and me, which is why I wanted to talk to you about something important."

"Are you sick?"

The fear in his eyes made me feel awful, and I rushed to assure him, "No, sweetie. Nothing bad like that, or at least I'm hoping you don't think it is."

"Then what did you want to talk about? Are you thinking about opening the store sooner?"

I couldn't let him keep making guesses. I needed to just get it out there. "How would you feel if I started dating?"

Simon shrugged. "I guess I'd be okay with that. I've always kind of wondered why you haven't already. Most of my friends with divorced parents had to deal with them dating super soon after they split up. I figured it's probably different because you didn't divorce Dad. He died."

I had to be very careful with my reply because I didn't want to lie to him. "Yes, my situation was different. But it's been just you and me for a long time. I'd understand if you need to think about this."

"Now that I'm going to be sixteen, I won't be around as much since I'll have my license. Plus, it won't be long until I leave for college. It would suck to think about you being lonely without me. I want you to be happy."

My boy was so sweet. "It's my job to worry about you, kiddo."

"I get to worry about you, too. I'm the man of the house, Mom." There was a mischievous gleam in his eyes as he added, "Which means I get to look over the guys you want to date, the same way you always do whenever I have a crush on a girl."

"About that..." I trailed off, my cheeks filling with heat as I tried to figure out how to tell him someone was already in my life.

"Oh, I see. This isn't you telling me you're *thinking* about dating. There's already a guy, isn't there?"

I nodded. "Yes, there is."

"Is it anyone I know? Please tell me it's not Garrett's dad."

My nose wrinkled. "Why would you think it's him?"

"Garrett called you a MILF the other day." Simon made a gagging noise. "When I threatened to kick his butt for talking about you like that, he told me that he was just repeating what he'd heard his dad say about you."

I made a mental note to avoid the guy. I could just imagine Baxter's reaction to him if he tried flirting with me. "It isn't him."

"Who is it?"

"Baxter Moore."

He blinked slowly. "The guy who bought Dad's SUV for me?"

I nodded. "Yup."

"Wow, I guess I can't complain too much about him then." He shrugged. "He seemed like a nice enough guy."

"You should bring him to one of my games when the season starts. Then Garrett's dad won't get any ideas in his head about asking you out. Garrett can be kind of a jerk sometimes, but I'd hate to lose him as a friend because I needed to kick his butt." His expression brightened. "But at least I'd have Baxter to help me take care of his dad."

I gave him my best mom glare. "That's enough talk about butt kicking."

"Sure thing." Then he spoiled his quick agreement by adding, "But I should probably point out that by not saying that Baxter wouldn't help me with Garrett's dad, you said an awful lot."

He was right, and the message I'd made by not saying anything was all true.

I smiled as Skylar whirled around me, her body dancing from side to side with jerky movements. She definitely wasn't too drunk to function, but she'd certainly had enough liquid courage to let her open up a bit. I loved seeing her so free, without all the constraints she normally put on herself. Dragging her to my Bentley, I buckled her in and kissed her on her forehead, eliciting a round of giggles from her.

As I came around to my side of the car, I laughed as well. I just couldn't help it. Although I'd had to wait five days after she called to let me know her son had given us the thumbs-up, our night of dinner and dancing had been perfect, and now I got to take her home with me until morning. I can't remember the last time I'd truly been so happy. Her hand slid up my thigh, grabbing and squeezing the muscles on her way up to the destination we both wanted her to reach. But right now, with me driving my most precious cargo, I didn't want that sort of distraction.

"I want you," she murmured, her husky tone almost eaten up by the roar of the engine.

I pulled her hand away and engulfed it in mine, giving her a small squeeze. "I want you, too. When we get to the house, I'm going to strip every inch of you naked and have my wicked way with you." I turned for a moment and winked at her, causing her to start giggling again.

"Oh, no you're not. This time, *I'm* going to have my way with *you*. You've done nothing but pleasure me. I think it's about time I reciprocated. Don't you?"

My cock pulsed at her words. I hated how confined I felt behind these pants. Luckily for me, my house wasn't that far. She had hinted and teased about pleasuring me, but now, with a bolster from the alcohol, she made no question about what she intended to do. Though I thoroughly loved getting her off, if she was so adamant about giving me the same courtesy, who was I to deny her that pleasure?

The moment we parked, she was on me like a

woman possessed. She unbuckled and launched herself over the gearshift to get at me, her lips pressing against mine with a hunger that rivaled my own. Grabbing the back of her head, I slanted my mouth against hers and kissed her, my tongue sliding across the seam of her lips to demand entrance.

When she opened for me, her tongue did the demanding. She thrust it deep inside, sliding in and out with unpracticed movements. I let her, allowing her to take the lead right now. Once she had her fill, I would take control again. Pink spread across her face as she pulled back, her grin widening as she looked at me in the dim light of the car interior.

"Let's get you inside."

She didn't have to ask me twice. Unbuckling, I exited my side and went around to open her door. She took my outstretched hand and stumbled out, her movements still a bit shaky. Though I wanted to carry her inside, I had a feeling it was important for her to be the aggressor right now. So I tamped down the caveman urge to just throw her over my shoulder and have my way with her. There was more than enough time for that later.

As we made our way inside, I barely had enough time to turn on the light when she tackled me, pinning me against the wall as her hot mouth slid up the side of my neck. My balls tightened as she ground up against me, her hips rubbing against my erection. If she kept up this teasing, I'd have no choice but to take control again and order her to satisfy me.

Groaning, it was my turn to let my head thump against the wall as she sank to her knees and fiddled with my belt. It felt like it took forever, but in reality, probably only ten seconds had passed. Soon, my pants were inching down, her hungry fingers grazing over the bare skin she revealed. Skylar tugged on my boxer briefs, finally allowing my erection to spring free.

The skin was so sensitive that even just her blowing on my tip made my hard shaft bob up in front of her. Precome pearled up at my slit, which she lapped up with more enthusiasm than I thought was possible. Her tongue was magic as it danced about, licking here and lapping there. I desperately wanted to grab her by the hair and force her mouth onto my cock, but I restrained myself. Once again, this was about Skylar and her pleasure. Maybe we could try something like that one day, but for right now, I was willingly at her mercy.

"Your tongue feels so good on me, beautiful."

My raspy compliment emboldened her. When Skylar's mouth opened above me, I shot up several prayers of gratitude to the heavens. Her mouth was a warm haven as she took me in and sucked. Moaning, I rocked into her, murmuring nonsensical adorations as she took me even deeper. I wasn't expecting her to deep-throat me. If it happened, amazing. If it didn't, I would be grateful for anything she did. Just having her touch me was more than enough.

She grazed her fingers across my balls, sending another jerk of pleasure up my shaft. When her grip tightened as she cupped them, my eyes rolled back into my head. Her mouth inched down a bit more as she took me deeper inside, her other hand massaging my balls until I thought I would come right there on the spot. "Oh, fuck. You've already got me so close."

As usual with this woman, all thoughts fled my brain. I took pride in reducing her to a babbling mess of need and want, and here she was doing the same thing to me. Grunting, I rocked into her, reveling in the sensation of her tongue and mouth working me over. My fingers slid into her hair, but I kept my grip light, still allowing her to control everything.

"God, beautiful," I moaned. "Your mouth feels so fucking good."

Skylar pulled back and rewarded me with a grin

so dazzling that it punched me in the gut. She was such a treasure. I stared in awe as I watched her go back to blowing me. Watching my cock disappear into her mouth was more erotic than anything I'd ever seen before. One of her hands gripped my thigh while the other circled the base of my shaft. As she stroked her hand in time with the bobbing of her head, I knew I wouldn't be able to last much longer.

Tingles started up my spine and flowed up and down my body as she pumped me in and out of her. My balls tightened even more, alerting me to how close I really was. My shaft pulsed as her tongue slid up the underside and around the tip.

"I'm going to come soon. If you don't want me in your mouth, you better pull away." My words were harried, gasping, and almost incoherent. I pressed against the wall, waiting for her to pull away, but she didn't. Instead, she shuffled closer, her lips sealing around me as she sucked.

My hand left her hair and slammed against the wall as her lips ripped the orgasm out of me, straight from my soul. "Fuuuck!" I rocked back and forth as Skylar took every bit of my essence into her mouth. Though I wasn't deep enough to feel her throat convulsing as she swallowed, I didn't have to. Her lips and tongue quivered around me as took in every drop.

Once I was clean, she pulled away, her eyes glassy with contentment. "Woman. You have five seconds to get your ass to my room before I fuck you here in this entryway."

The sassy look she shot me as she ambled to her feet sent another twitch through my softening cock. "One," she teased, holding up a finger as she backed away slowly.

"Two," I growled as I peeled myself away from the wall. Easing my feet out of my pants, I left them there by the door, not caring at all about the mess at that moment.

"Three?" Her voice was a soft squeak as she took another step away from me.

"Four." I straightened up to my full height and took another step forward, eating the distance between us. When she didn't move again, I leaned down and looked her straight in the eyes. "Five."

At that word, she burst into a flurry of motion, racing before me to get to the bedroom. I stared in wonder as her body quivered with excitement. Though I had just been sucked dry, my cock was already at half-mast as I began the chase. This woman was going to be the death of me but in the best way possible.

By the time I made it to the bedroom, she was already stripped out of her clothes and waiting for me on the bed. A soft growl reverberated in my throat as I stared at her beautiful form just waiting there for me. Her eyes went from my face to my rigid cock, a look of bewilderment passing over her features.

If it helped her, I was bewildered too. This was a fast recovery period for me. "What can I say?" I smirked, padding over to the bed. "I have a beautiful woman who just snatched my soul with her mouth, and I want nothing more than to fuck her over and over again." Sliding my palm across her cheek, I bent down and gave her a soft kiss. "I just can't get enough of you."

I crawled next to her on the soft sheets and kissed her a bit more thoroughly. I wasn't kidding when I said I couldn't get enough. Even though I left the heat of her mouth just minutes ago, I needed her again. Reaching over to the drawer, I grabbed one of the condoms and tore at the wrapping while our lips were still fused together. Rolling it down my shaft, I slid my hands down to Skylar's hips and gripped her before flipping her over.

Her ass was a thing of beauty. Bending low, I skimmed my lips across one cheek then the other, noting the explosion of goose bumps over her body. She was so wet. Even in the dim light, I saw just how much she glistened with arousal. Unable to deny our mutual need anymore, I lined up my cock with her and surged home.

"So fucking perfect," I growled as Skylar cried out, her pussy gripping me as I sank deep inside her tight channel. God, but she wanted this just as much as I did. Reaching around, I strummed my fingers against her clit. The main benefit to already coming was that I could last a bit longer as she found her pleasure. I slammed into her, changing up my angle based on the noises she made.

Soon, her fingers were digging into the sheets as she rocked back against me. "Right there, huh? Is that where you want my cock, beautiful?"

"Yes," she gasped.

Though it took all my willpower, I stayed still behind her, letting her find her rhythm. Soon, her body rippled around mine, and I started pounding into her once more, riding out her orgasm as I found mine. Her moans filled my ears as my fingers clenched and relaxed around her hips.

I drank them in, using them as fuel to light the

fire on my own climax. With a loud shout, I came, my hips jerking in an erratic rhythm as I filled the condom. Groaning, I pulled Skylar close, refusing to let her go until I absolutely had to. Minutes went by, and my cock finally started to soften, satisfied at last.

Pulling out, I rolled her onto her side and kissed her temple, whispering how amazing she was. I left her there, blissed out as I cleaned up. I didn't want to be away from her for too long, not when I finally had her in my bed for the night. Taking a warm rag, I went back into the bedroom.

She looked incredible, her hair tousled and mussed, fanned out over my pillow...like she belonged there. How I wanted her to stay there more than just tonight, but that would be moving things far too fast. Tonight, though. At least I had tonight. If we were going to talk about us together for longer, I wanted to do it when she was sober and could really grasp what I was asking for.

Skylar was far more important to me than I realized. Seeing her here, I just couldn't imagine her anywhere else. Pulling back my side of the covers, I helped her under and dragged her warm body next to mine. Something just felt so right about her in my arms. I hugged her close, turning her so that her head rested on my chest. Her soft breaths stirred the skin below, and happiness filled my soul.

"I have to be up early," she whispered, sadness lacing her tone.

"That's still hours away." I didn't want to think about her leaving in the morning while I cleaned her up. "Stay right here."

Tearing myself away from her, I walked back to my pants so I could grab my phone. Then I headed down to the kitchen and grabbed two bottles of water, along with some painkillers from the supplies I kept there. Soon, those drinks would catch up with her.

I padded back into the room, my cock stirring once more at the sight of her lying in my bed. I would never get enough of that. I set the bottles and pain meds down on the nightstand closest to her and set my alarm for six o'clock. As much as I didn't want her to go, I knew she needed to be home when Simon came back from his friend's house before they went to church.

With my alarm set, even if we fell asleep, I could still get her up and back to her house. I didn't like it, but I understood. Slipping back into the bed, I pulled her close, breathing her scent deep into my lungs. She was so soft and warm. I wanted nothing more than to just keep her here with me forever but now was not the time. Hopefully soon, even though things were moving lightning fast between us now that we were together. Until Skylar, I'd never been one to patiently wait when I found something I wanted.

"Happy Birthday," I cried when Simon walked into the kitchen a week later.

He slid onto one of the stools at the counter. "Thanks, Mom."

As soon as I heard him go into the bathroom upstairs, I had started making his favorite breakfast. After sliding the plate in front of him, I waved my hands in the air. "Ta-da! French toast with sliced strawberries and powdered sugar. Just how you like it. Plus, extra crispy bacon and maple breakfast sausage links."

"Looks good," he muttered, grabbing his fork and knife to dig into the French toast.

I thought for sure he would be in a great mood this morning. He'd been excited about getting his license ever since he'd gone for his learner's permit, and today was the big day. I'd hoped between that and his birthday, he'd pull out of the funk he'd been in for the past several days.

I'd also thought he'd come to me with whatever was bothering him, but so far, he'd done his best to avoid deep conversations with me. "Are you nervous about the driving test?"

"Yeah, a little, I guess." He shrugged as he took a sip of his orange juice. "But it's not that big of a deal. Mike didn't pass his first time, and he only had to wait like one day before he could take the test again."

I'd actually looked up the rules, but I didn't want to tell him that because I didn't want him to think I didn't have faith in how he was going to do today. "That's good, buddy. One day isn't too bad, but I bet you won't even have to worry about retaking the test. You'll nail it the first time around."

"Yeah, last time I went out with Grandpa, he said I was an even better driver than Dad was when he was my age." His shoulders slumped. "And he only had to take the test once, so I should be fine."

I would've expected he'd feel encouraged by that fact, but he seemed even more bummed out. Circling around the counter, I patted him on the back. "You'll be better than fine."

"I hope so," he grumbled before shoving half a sausage link into his mouth.

I got the message loud and clear—he didn't want to talk about it. Not wanting to make him more nervous, I let the matter drop and got busy cleaning up the mess I made so I'd be ready to go when he was done. We took my car since he'd driven it more often than the SUV, and I gave him a quick peck on the cheek before I slid out of the passenger door. "Good luck, sweetie."

I paced back and forth in front of the Bureau of Motor Vehicles office while he was doing the road test, twisting my hands together. He was only gone for about half an hour, but it felt like forever until he returned to the parking lot. As they climbed out of the car, the examiner was smiling, so I assumed all went well. This was confirmed when he greeted me. "Hello, Mrs. Hicks. Simon did great. If you'll head inside with him, it shouldn't be too long before they call your name to get his permit swapped out with his license."

The little celebratory dance I did got me a brief chuckle from Simon before we followed the examiner's instructions. About half an hour later, when we walked back out to my car with his license in his wallet, he didn't seem any happier than he'd been at breakfast. When we pulled into our driveway and I saw his SUV parked in front of the garage, I thought maybe taking it for a drive by himself for the first time might cheer him up. "Do you have your keys?"

He nodded. "Yup."

"How about I start on your usual chores as an extra birthday gift, and you go for a little drive," I suggested. "Just try to be back in an hour or so because people will be popping in and out today to drop off gifts and wish you a happy birthday."

"Sure, I guess so."

I reached for his arm before he climbed out of my car. "If driving your dad's SUV brings back too many memories, you can use mine instead. We'll swap vehicles, easy peasy."

"No, I don't want to do that." He shook his head emphatically. "You're better off in your car."

My eyes narrowed as I tried to figure out why my offer seemed to upset him. "Is there something wrong with the SUV? Do we need to take it to the mechanic so they can take a look?"

"No, it runs fine." He flashed me a weak smile. "Everything's okay, Mom. Don't worry. I'll be back before anyone shows up. I promise."

I heaved a deep sigh as I watched him back out of the driveway in the SUV. As soon as he was gone, I ran inside and started to put up decorations. He'd said he didn't want a big party this year, but that didn't mean we weren't going to celebrate. No way was I going to allow his sixteenth birthday to pass by without at least doing something special for him.

As promised, I had Simon's chores done when he returned about an hour later. He was just in time for a few of his friends to stop by with cards for him. They stayed to munch on snacks I put out and watched a movie in the basement. Shortly after they left, his grandparents dropped off their present and promised to take him out to dinner at his favorite steak place next weekend. After they left, I gave him the card my parents had sent, along with a few gifts from me—a gamer headset, the new gaming console that just came out last month, and a "Don't do stupid shit" keychain. As happy as he was with the gaming stuff, it was the keychain that got the best reaction—genuine laughter.

It was late afternoon when Baxter stopped by. I'd tried to convince him that he didn't need to get Simon a birthday gift since he'd technically already bought him a vehicle, but he refused to listen to reason. At least he'd agreed not to spend anything more than I had, though the two presents he was carrying looked awfully fancy.

"Hey, beautiful," he greeted as he walked into the house, brushing a quick kiss against my cheek. "Where's the birthday boy?"

"Right here," Simon answered as he walked out of the kitchen. "I was just polishing off a big chunk of the chocolate sheet cake Mom made for me before Aunt Sarah shows up with an even bigger cake."

Baxter grinned at him. "Double cake sounds like a great birthday to me."

"Yeah, Aunt Sarah can do some fancy stuff with a cake, but nothing beats Mom's chocolate sheet cake."

"I'd have to agree."

Simon stretched his arm out to shake Baxter's hand. "Thanks for stopping by to celebrate my birthday with us, Mr. Moore."

"As long as it's okay with your mom, you can call me Baxter."

They both gave me an expectant look, and I nodded. "It's totally fine by me."

Baxter held one of the presents out to Simon. "I hope it's okay that I come bearing gifts."

"Seeing as you're dating my mom, I guess I'll allow it," Simon teased.

Baxter chuckled. "Thanks."

We moved into the living room, Simon claiming

the recliner while Baxter sat next to me on the couch before he opened his presents. The first was four tickets to a Chicago Cubs game next month. "Your mom mentioned how much you love baseball. I checked your team's schedule to make sure you weren't playing that day. I figured your mom and I could take you and a friend to the game. Just a quick trip there and back, all in the same day. Unless your mom and your friend's parents decide it'll be better if we stay overnight instead. Whatever works best for you guys is fine by me."

The awe in my son's eyes made me sniffle but in the very best way possible. Baxter had gotten him the perfect gift, but even better, he'd known exactly what to get him because he listened to everything I told him.

"Are we gonna drive up or take the helicopter?" Simon asked, still staring at the tickets.

"We can take the helicopter if you want and your mom says it's okay."

"Cool," Simon breathed.

"I also got you an advanced copy of this." Baxter handed him another present. "I thought maybe we could play it together since there's a multiplayer option."

Simon ripped into the wrapping paper, his eyes

widening and his jaw going slack at the baseball game that wasn't due to be released for another two months. "You play video games?"

A hint of red hit his cheeks. "Yeah."

"Wanna give this a try now?" Simon asked.

"Sure."

I trailed them with a big smile. Seeing Baxter and Simon interact melted my heart. They played the new baseball game for about an hour before Baxter had to leave. As I walked him to the door, I whispered, "You so earned yourself another blow job."

"Didn't do it to get brownie points with you, beautiful." He pressed his lips against my ear. "But I sure as fuck am not going to turn down the chance to feel your pretty lips wrapped around my cock again."

My pussy throbbed at the heat in his voice, and I stood there in a sensual daze for a good ten minutes after he left. It wasn't until my best friend let herself into the house that I shook myself out of it. "Hey, Sarah."

I heard Simon pause his game and then his footsteps pounding on the stairs from the basement. "The cake looks great. Thanks, Aunt Sarah."

"Glad you like it." My best friend looked over her shoulder as Simon stomped through the living room toward the kitchen. Her voice was low as she asked, "What's up with the birthday boy? He doesn't seem super excited for someone who just got his license, has his own car, and has the extra-special deliciousness I baked for him to look forward to for dessert."

"Your guess is as good as mine." I scrubbed my hands down my face. "He's been acting weird all week."

Her gaze turned considering. "Ever since you talked to him about the sexy billionaire?"

I rolled my eyes. "Are you ever going to just use his name? Because it'll be awfully embarrassing to have you refer to him as the sexy billionaire when you meet him."

"Things must be going well if you're thinking about putting him up to the best friend challenge." She flashed me a mischievous grin.

I wagged my finger at her. "And that right there is why you'll probably be the last to get to know him."

"Relax, Skylar. I promise not to embarrass you... too much." Her shoulders shook as she giggled. "But seriously, you don't need to worry about me putting him to the test. As far as I'm concerned, he's earned the stamp of approval for making you come alive again. And that's not even taking into consideration all the pretty pink roses, romantic picnic, indoor skydiving, dinner and dancing, and your first helicopter ride. But are you worried that Simon has changed his mind?"

My brows drew together as I thought about when I first noticed something off with my son. Shaking my head, I murmured, "I don't think that's the problem. He teased me about spending the night at Baxter's when he got home from his sleepover. It wasn't until the next day that his dark mood descended upon our house. And he was better than he'd been in days when Baxter stopped by to drop off a present for him earlier."

"It's a milestone birthday. Maybe he's just missing his dad more than usual?" she suggested.

I hoped she was right, but I couldn't shake the feeling that something more was going on with my son.

Seeing Skylar's name on my phone screen made me smile. "Hey, do you have any big plans today?" she asked before I had the chance to say hello.

Considering it was my birthday, my answer should have been yes. But it wasn't. "Even if I did, you know I would change them in a heartbeat for you. Spending time with you is the best offer I can get."

Laughter drifted through the phone line. "I'm sure that's not true, but I'm glad you think so. It bodes well for our relationship in the future."

I loved when she made offhand comments about being with me long term because I planned to spend the rest of my life with her. It was still much too early to pop the question—we hadn't used the four-letter L-word out loud with each other yet—but I'd already bought the ring I planned to slide onto her finger at some point in the future. As my grandfather had told me when I asked him how he'd known my grandmother was the one for him—when you know, you know. It was as simple and complicated as that.

"What did you have in mind?"

"I was hoping you'd stop by my house."

"Any particular time?"

"Whenever you can get here works for me."

I stood and slid my wallet in the back pocket of my jeans before grabbing the keys to my truck. "How about now?"

"Now would be great."

My day was definitely looking up. I whistled to myself as I strode into the garage. The trip to Skylar's house was quick, and one I'd made a few times over the past couple of weeks. She and Simon had me over for dinner one night, and I'd picked her up for a date on another. I had also spent a couple more hours playing video games with Simon. He was such a great kid, and I was lucky he'd been okay with me dating his mom because it was impossible to miss how much she loved him. I loved that she was the kind of person who'd do just about anything for her son. It was so different from what I'd grown up with.

When I pulled into Skylar's driveway, she was waiting on her front step. "Hey, beautiful."

"C'mon, I have something for you." She interlaced our fingers and led me into the house and toward the kitchen, where a familiar-looking pan sat on the counter.

"You made me a chocolate sheet cake?"

She nodded. "A little birdie told me it was your birthday tomorrow."

My mouth was dry, and I had to wet my lips before I explained, "Sorry I didn't share that with you myself, beautiful. I wasn't sure how I was going to feel about celebrating this year. My last birthday was tough because it wasn't that long after we lost Weston."

"Oh." Her smile wavered, and there was a worried gleam in her beautiful eyes. "It's okay if you want to skip your birthday this year. You don't need to eat the cake just because I baked it for you."

"It isn't just any cake." I dipped a finger into the frosting. "It's the same one you made for me right after we met."

"You said you ate all of that one, and it's one of the few cake recipes I'm any good at making from scratch. Doing a cake from the box the first time we're celebrating your birthday together didn't seem right."

I'd been pleased when she'd shown up on my doorstep with a cake, but my reaction paled compared to how it felt knowing that she'd baked this one in honor of my birthday. The same kind of cake she'd made for her much-loved son. It made me feel damn special. "Like I told Simon on his birthday, nothing beats your chocolate sheet cake."

"You didn't actually say that. He did. You just agreed," she pointed out.

I brushed a kiss against her cheek. "Doesn't make it any less true."

"Good, then maybe it'll help brighten your birthday."

"It definitely does." I dipped my finger in the frosting again, sucking the digit clean before I claimed her mouth. "Almost as much as being with you."

Her voice was breathless as she asked, "Is that so?"

"Abso-fucking-lutely. You're always the best part of my day, beautiful."

I loved how my simple compliment made her gorgeous blue eyes light up with happiness. "Then maybe I can convince you to let me cook dinner for you tonight?"

I couldn't think of a better way to celebrate my birthday than to share a meal with the woman I'd fallen for. "It wouldn't take any convincing at all."

"Good." She beamed a smile at me. "Because I already bought all the stuff to make you my mom's famous bacon-wrapped pork tenderloin with roasted vegetables."

I patted my stomach. "That sounds amazing."

"What's your opinion on dessert before your meal?"

I pretended to consider her question for a moment before I nodded. "I'm definitely in favor of it."

"Fantastic." She clapped her hands together. "I'll cut you a slice now."

While she was doing that, I noticed how quiet the house was. "Where's Simon?"

"He's running some errands for me. Him having a license and his own vehicle sure does come in handy sometimes." She arched her brow. "Like when you need to do some emergency birthday shopping."

I grimaced. "Sorry, beautiful. Even if I wasn't sure that I wanted to celebrate, I still should've let you know it was my birthday."

"That's okay. I really do get it, and that'll be the last time I poke at you for the oversight." She handed me a plate with a big chunk of cake on it. "Simon wanted to get you something, too. He thought it was pretty cool that your birthdays are so close together."

"Maybe we'll make the trip to Chicago for a Cubs game an annual birthday thing." I followed her into the living room, taking a bite of my cake along the way.

"I think he'd really like that."

I'd managed to snag club box seats between the dugouts only a few rows back from the field this time around, but I decided to look into the suite options they offered for next year. If we made the trip a tradition, Simon might enjoy experiencing the different views Wrigley Field had to offer. "And what about you? Would you like it, too?"

"You being sweet and treating my boy to something he loves while you two do some male bonding?" she asked, her voice as soft as her expression. "Yeah, I'd love that."

If I hadn't already liked the idea, I would've been on board just to put the look on her face. I didn't think anyone had ever called me sweet before Skylar. But I'd never put in the same kind of effort with anyone else. Everything was different with her, including me. Being with Skylar made me a better man. And so fucking thankful that I'd moved to Mooreville. If I hadn't, I never would've met her, and that would've been a damn shame. In a strange twist of fate, I owed my current happiness to my brother. I only wished Weston was here to see it.

"You and Simon make it easy to be sweet, beautiful."

"Seriously, stop." She sniffled. "I shouldn't cry on your birthday, but if you keep it up, that's exactly what I'm going to do. Happy tears, though."

I set my plate on the end table and bent toward Skylar. "How about I give you something better to do than cry, even if they're happy tears?"

Her smile was shaky, and her gorgeous blue eyes glistened with those tears she'd warned me about. "What did you have in mind?"

"Come a little closer, and I'll show you," I urged, wrapping my arm around her shoulders to pull her against my side.

Pressing her hand against my chest, she tilted her head back and smiled up at me. "That sounds like an offer I don't want to pass up."

"Thank fuck," I murmured against her lips before I pressed my mouth against hers. With our tongues tangling, I wrapped her hair around my fist to bring her head farther back so I could deepen our kiss.

Her eyes were hazy with passion when I pulled back to stare into them. "Mmm, you taste like chocolate cake."

"Maybe you should get a better sample." I gripped her waist to urge her onto my lap.

"Good idea," she agreed, swinging a leg over so she could straddle me. When she dropped down fully onto my lap, the heat from her pussy scorched my already rock-hard dick. I wrapped one of my arms around her back to press her closer, taking great pleasure in the feel of her hard nipples grazing against my chest, even through two layers of clothes.

Our kiss quickly spiraled out of control, and I was just thinking about asking her how long Simon would be gone when I heard the sound of an engine coming close. The mental birthday wish I sent up that it would continue past the house wasn't answered.

Ripping my mouth from Skylar's, I lifted her off my lap and sat her on the cushion next to me. Her eyes were hazy with passion as she puffed out her bottom lip in a pout. "Why'd you stop?"

I jerked my chin toward the front door. "I think

Simon is back. I heard a car door slam, and it sounded like it came from your driveway."

"Oh, crap." She smoothed down the front of her shirt. "It's a good thing you heard him. Although he's on board with us dating, I'm sure he doesn't want to walk in on us making out."

As soon as the words were out of her mouth, Simon stormed in the house and stalked toward us.

"I don't care how rich he is. You need to kick him to the curb." The betrayal in his blue eyes, so much like Skylar's, was a punch to the gut. "He's a cheater, Mom."

*What in the literal fuck was happening?* I'd never cheated on a woman, and I sure as hell wasn't going to start with the only one I'd ever loved.

My head was spinning. I wanted to give Baxter my trust, but Simon seemed so certain of what he was saying. And I'd been wrong before. "Why do you think Baxter is cheating on me?"

"Because his fiancée said so." His chin jerked up. "And she didn't have any reason to lie about it. Unlike him."

"Fiancée?" I echoed softly, turning toward Baxter, who looked as shocked as I felt. "You said you never even came close to getting married before."

"Because I haven't," he insisted with a shake of his head. "The only jewelry I've ever bought for a woman was a bracelet as a token of my appreciation when I ended things. Until you. And that was a damn long time ago."

His ring wasn't on my finger, but that sounded an awful lot like he was saying that he'd already got me one. I couldn't go there right now, though. Not with the verbal bomb Simon had just dropped. "Then why is some woman going up to my son and calling herself your fiancée?"

"I don't know," he gritted out, his nostrils flaring. "But you can be damn sure I'm going to find out."

Having this conversation in front of my son was all kinds of wrong, but it couldn't be avoided when he was smack dab in the middle of this mess. "You really have no idea who it could be?"

"I have never, not once, cheated on a woman. I sure as heck am not going to start now, when I've finally found the one I plan on spending the rest of my life with."

There wasn't anything vague about that statement and no mistaking what he meant. He'd just thrown his intention to marry me right out there...at the worst time possible. Even with the ugly accusation my son had thrown out, butterflies swirled in my belly at the thought of becoming Baxter's wife. But I couldn't focus on the possibility that we'd somehow be able to wade through this disaster and find ourselves on the other side together. Simon came first, even when my heart was breaking—a lesson his father had taught me after he died.

"Don't listen to him, Mom. You can't trust him."

Turning to my son, I reached out to take his hand in mine. "I'm not sure who this woman was or why she'd say something like that, but Baxter hasn't given us any reason to believe his word isn't good. I think he's earned the right to give us his side of the story, don't you?"

A hint of vulnerability seeped into Simon's eyes as he shook his head. "You thought you could trust Dad, and look how that turned out."

My other hand flew to my chest, and my knees almost gave out. It took every ounce of my self-control to stay on my feet as I gaped at my son. "What do you mean, sweetie?"

"I mean that you don't need another man who is going to treat you like crap by cheating on you. You deserve more."

"Another?" My mind was already reeling. Finding out that my son had somehow discovered his father's infidelity was almost more than I could bear.

"Yeah, I know Dad was a cheater, too."

Straightening my spine, I turned toward the man who'd crept behind my protective walls and claimed my heart for himself. "I'm sorry, Baxter. I know we're in the middle of something that could have a huge impact on our relationship, but I need to ask you to leave."

"Skylar, no." He shook his head, a muscle jumping in his jaw. "Please, we need to talk this out. Don't make me go."

I walked over to the door and wrapped my hand around the knob. Before I pulled it open, I looked at him over my shoulder. I hated how defeated he looked. Under different circumstances, I would have wrapped my arms around his broad shoulders and held him close. But I couldn't bring myself to touch him when the specter of the woman who'd claimed to be his fiancée was hanging over our heads. "We will talk about this, but later. My son needs me right now."

Baxter shoved his hands in his pockets before moving closer to Simon. "I know you're hurting right now, but I swear I'm going to fix this. I would not have asked you how you felt about me marrying your mom sometime in the future if I didn't know deep down in my soul that I'd be able to treat both of you right."

What a way to find out Baxter had talked to my son about wanting to marry me.

Simon glared at him. "The only way you can fix this is if you can prove that woman was lying and you're not. Otherwise, you can take that blessing you asked me for and shove it up your ass. And while you're at it, you can take back the SUV, too. My approval isn't for sale."

Baxter rocked back on his heels. "Don't make any hasty decisions while you're upset, kiddo. If you still feel the same after I've proven to you, I'll take the SUV. But I'll store it in my garage in case you change your mind later when you aren't quite so angry with your dad anymore."

He looked as ravaged as I felt when he turned to walk toward the door I was holding open. Keeping his hands in his pockets, he paused at my side. "While you're working things out with your boy, I'll be getting to the bottom of this. Whoever hurt him will pay. I swear it to you, beautiful."

His vow seemed sincere, and I hoped like heck he was telling the truth.

After the door shut behind Baxter, I led Simon over to the couch. We both sat down, and I patted his hand. "How did you find out what happened with your dad?"

His shoulders slumped, and I hated how sad he was. This was why I never wanted him to know about Steven's affair. "I found a note wedged under the back seat when I was cleaning out the SUV again like a week before I went for my driving test."

"That explains why you've been quieter than usual." I pinched the bridge of my nose between my thumb and forefinger, trying my best to stop myself from crying. "Why didn't you say anything to me before now?"

"I wasn't sure if you knew, and I didn't want to be the one who told you what Dad did." His eyes narrowed. "He couldn't hurt you anymore, but the same isn't true for Baxter. I had to tell you what happened with that lady in town so you wouldn't fall for his lies and end up even more hurt than you are right now. She didn't even know who I was or that I was eavesdropping."

"My sweet baby boy." I leaned close and pressed my lips against his forehead. "Looking out for his mom."

He ducked his head, his cheeks filling with heat at my compliment. "Someone has to do it."

"I'm so lucky to have you." I bumped my shoulder against his. "But let's set the situation with Baxter aside for a moment. First, we need to talk about your dad and how you feel about what you learned."

His Adam's apple bobbed in his throat as his bottom lip trembled. "I, um, I don't get how he could do something like that to us."

"I can understand why you'd feel betrayed, but you need to know that your dad loved you very much, and nothing would have ever changed that," I assured him with a soft smile.

He jumped up to pace back and forth in front of the couch. "Then why would he do something that could blow up our family?"

If only I had a definitive answer for that question, I might've been able to come to terms with everything much sooner. But Steven had already been dead when I found out about his indiscretion, so I hadn't been able to ask him what the heck he'd been thinking. "I'm not sure, Simon. But one thing I do know is that he never would've wanted to hurt you."

"But he did," my son cried.

"Everyone makes mistakes," I reminded him.

"It's how we handle them that counts," he echoed what Steven and I told him whenever he got into trouble.

"Unfortunately, your dad never got the chance to make amends for this mistake."

Simon dropped onto the couch with a sigh,

scrubbing his hands down his face. "I don't see how he could come back from something as big as this."

"Some mistakes are bigger than others, and we don't think about the consequences until it's too late." I took a cleansing breath, surprised by how calm I was discussing something that I'd barely been able to think about without wanting to cry only a few months ago. "But I have no doubt that your father would've figured out how to make this up to you. He wouldn't have stopped until he earned back your trust and rebuilt his relationship with you."

His voice was barely audible as he asked, "And you would've been okay with that?"

"Absolutely." I reached out to squeeze his forearm. "I would've done whatever it took to help him."

He sniffled. "Even if you hated him because of what he did?"

"I could never hate your dad. Not really." Although I'd come darn close for a very long time. "No matter how angry I was with him, he still gave me the best thing that ever happened to me—you."

His lips curved into a small smile. "I am pretty awesome."

"The awesomest," I agreed.

"So are you." This time, he bumped me with his

shoulder. "Which is why you deserve a guy who'll treat you right. Not someone who'll lie and cheat."

It didn't hit me until right then how much I trusted Baxter. And his family. Steven's cheating was kept secret because no one in town knew about it... except his parents.

I hadn't realized they were aware of what he'd been up to until about a month after his death when his mom asked me not to make them pay for the mistakes their son made. She'd been upset because they hadn't seen Simon since the funeral, and I had called to cancel an upcoming visit. They had thought my decision was because I was angry with them when the true reason was that he'd been struggling with abandonment issues and wasn't ready to be apart from me for more than a day.

Finding out that they had kept his cheating a secret from me had hurt just as bad as knowing about his infidelity. But I knew if Baxter really was engaged to some other woman, Dean never would have agreed to be his wingman. His family would rip him up one side and down another for being a cheater. No matter how much they loved him, they wouldn't let Baxter get away with something like that. And deep down inside, I knew he'd never even try. "Baxter does treat me right. There has to be an explanation for your encounter with that woman, no matter how unlikely it is for her to be the one who's lying."

I only hoped I hadn't damaged his trust in me by forcing him to leave without giving him a chance to help us figure out what had happened.

Walking out of Skylar's house was the hardest thing I've ever done. The pain in her eyes felt like a punch to the gut, and the accusation in Simon's wasn't any better. The last thing I wanted to do was leave in the middle of a fight, but I couldn't ignore Skylar's request. She needed time with her son to talk about how he found out about his dad cheating on her and whatever the hell had gone down with the woman who'd claimed she was my fiancée. She had to make sure he was okay before she could focus on our relationship.

Simon was her priority, and I respected the fuck out of her for it. But someone else was using her motherly instincts against us. They had tried to turn the boy against me, and they were going to pay for their mistake. I just had to figure out who the fuck they were first.

As I backed out of her driveway, I mulled over what Simon had said. I couldn't think of anyone in Mooreville who would try to pass themselves off as my fiancée. My relationship with Skylar was no secret, and everyone in town was rooting for us to make this thing work. Trying to break us up was a surefire way to earn a fuck ton of enemies, and most of them would have Moore for their last name. Which was imprudent considering the breadth and depth of the power my family held.

None of this made any sense...unless the person causing trouble was an outsider. But who in the hell would come all the way to Mooreville to interfere in my life?

Only one answer came to mind, but before I went straight to the source, I figured I could use more intel. Stabbing my finger against my cell phone's screen, I pulled up Rigden's number and called him.

I barely let him say hello before I barked, "Has your dad said anything about my parents coming to town?"

"What? No way," he denied. "And if Uncle Dan was planning on visiting Mooreville and my dad knew about it, he definitely would have said something. He wouldn't be able to keep big news like that to himself for long."

"Fuck, you're right," I grunted, slamming my palm against my steering wheel.

"Why in the hell did you think he'd deign to grace the residents of Mooreville with his presence after all this time?"

I gave him a quick rundown of what had just happened. When I was done, he let out a low whistle. "Shit, man. I'm sorry. You think your parents snuck into town and brought one of those socialites they kept throwing at you, thinking they could lure you back to the Big Apple?"

"I know how absurd it sounds, but nothing else makes sense." I heaved a deep sigh, shaking my head.

"Maybe we're looking at it the wrong way," Rigden suggested.

My brows drew together. "What do you mean?"

"What if there's a woman out there who actually believed the crap they spouted off to Simon?"

"That makes even less sense," I countered, shaking my head. "Why in the world would some woman think I was going to marry her when I hadn't been with anyone in more than a year before I moved? And I haven't so much as looked at another woman since I met Skylar."

"Maybe that's where your first guess comes into play," Rigden replied.

My knuckles turned white as I clenched the steering wheel. "You think my dad has something to do with this?"

"You haven't given anyone but Skylar reason to believe you'd slide your ring on their finger, but who knows what empty promises your parents have made on your behalf."

His suggestion should've been preposterous, but my mom had pulled some ridiculous stunts in the weeks leading up to my departure. And my dad hadn't done a damn thing to make her try to see reason. "I hate to admit it, but you might be on the right track. I'm gonna make a couple of calls and confirm my parents are still in New York."

"While you're doing that, I'll put some feelers out to see if anyone has spotted any outsiders in town," he offered.

"I appreciate anything you can do to shed some light on this clusterfuck."

It only took me fifteen minutes to drive to my office, and I had to stop myself from doing a U-turn at every single stoplight along the way. The farther away from Skylar's house I got, the less certain I was that I should've left. I understood why she'd asked me to go after the second verbal bomb Simon had dropped. She needed to talk to him about how he'd discovered his dad had cheated on her and help him work through what he was feeling about it.

I was sitting in my truck, idling at the curb while I stared at her shop when my phone rang. Assuming Rigden was calling me back, I didn't look at the screen as I accepted the call and was shocked when Skylar's voice came through the speakers. "Are you at home?"

"No, that felt like I'd be too far away from you. I'm parked in front of your shop."

"I am so sorry I didn't give you the chance to explain."

My head reared back. "What? No, Skylar. I don't need an apology for that. It was fucked-up timing, but Simon needed you. Is he okay?"

"That right there is why I shouldn't have asked you to leave." She sniffled, and I knew she was trying not to cry.

"The only thing I need from you right now is for you to tell me that you know I didn't cheat on you."

My breath caught in my chest while I waited for her answer. "I have no idea why some woman is walking around town saying she's engaged to you, but there has to be some explanation for it. Because you wouldn't cheat on me."

My hands dropped from the steering wheel as my entire body slumped forward. With what Skylar went through with her husband, it would have hurt like fuck, but I wouldn't have blamed her if she needed proof that I wasn't cheating. "Your trust is the best damn birthday present I've ever received."

"I'm glad you think so, but I hate that we had to go through whatever the heck this was today of all days."

A notification popped up on my phone. "Hold on a second, beautiful. Rigden was helping me figure out what happened, and he may have something for us."

I glanced at the screen to read the text message.

**Rigden:** I was apparently wrong about my dad. He can keep big news to himself. Your parents aren't here right now, but they're supposed to be in town tomorrow for a family dinner.

**Me:** Fuck.

**Rigden:** Yeah, my dad is beyond pissed. Their visit was supposed to be a birthday surprise. He had no idea they were going to pull shit that would fuck up your life.

**Me:** Tell him to back down. Let them come. They'll be the ones surprised in the end.

**Rigden:** Will do.

"Fucking hell," I groaned.

"Did he figure it out?" Skylar asked.

"Yeah, my parents are behind this."

"What?" she screeched. "Holy crap."

I wished that I shared her shock, but after their shitty reaction to Weston's death, nothing they did would surprise me anymore. "They're tomorrow's problem. Right now, I want to find whichever woman they sent here with promises of marrying me. Did Simon give you more details about what happened?"

"He was in that little menswear shop on Union, around the corner from Leaves & Pages. I noticed they had a tie that was the same shade as your eyes, and I asked him to pick it up for me so I could give it to you for your birthday," she explained.

I hopped out of my car, determined to find her even if I had to walk up and down the street all day.

"You want to see this happen, get your ass down here. I can't risk this woman leaving town before I have the chance to confront her."

"Simon and I are already in the car headed to you. We'll be there soon."

I loved that they were coming to me, but I wasn't sure about Simon being in the middle of this mess. Especially on the heels of his confession about knowing his dad cheated on his mom. "You sure you want Simon here for this?"

"Hold on a sec. I'm going to let him answer for himself."

She switched to speaker mode, and Simon's voice came through the line. "I'm fine. Not upset. Just pissed."

He sounded a lot better than he'd been when I left their house. "Are you sure?"

"Yeah, no way am I going to let Mom drive into town by herself when she's freaked out and wants to talk to you on the phone. She could get into an accident."

I squeezed my eyes shut at how his voice trembled at the end. All this shit must've dredged up the grief he'd felt when his dad died. "Thank you for taking such good care of your mom."

"I need you to do the same. Please be the guy she thinks you are. I'd hate to have to kick your butt."

Skylar's startled laugh before she hissed his name made me smile. "I'll do my best to make sure that never has to happen."

"Good."

I spotted a familiar face a few blocks down just as they parked behind my truck. After I opened Skylar's door and helped her out of the car, I pointed in the woman's direction. "Does that look like her?"

Simon peered down the street, his eyes going wide before he nodded. "Yeah, she's wearing the same outfit."

"C'mon." I interlaced my fingers with Skylar's and practically dragged her down the street while Simon followed closely behind. When we got close, I called, "Tinsley Sheridan, is that you?"

The pampered socialite whirled around, her eyes going wide when she saw me, and then narrowing when she noticed I was holding Skylar's hand. "Indeed, it is. Happy Birthday, Baxter. Surprise!"

"Surprise?" I echoed softly, pulling Skylar closer as Simon moved to stand on her other side.

"You came to Mooreville because it's my birthday?"

"Yes, I wanted to surprise you at dinner

tomorrow night." Her lips formed a circle, and she pressed her fingers to her mouth. "Oh dear, and now I've ruined the surprise. I suppose it would've been better if I had flown back to New York so I could travel with your parents, but it seemed like such a bother when I was on the West Coast. I came directly here instead."

I ground my teeth together at her confirmation that my parents were to blame for this mess. "Now that the surprise has been ruined, maybe you could explain to me why you've been going around town calling yourself my fiancée."

"Well...I couldn't stay in my hotel room until your parents arrived. The place is seriously lacking in amenities, so I thought I'd do a little shopping." She seemed to finally realize how angry I was, and her voice wavered as she tried to explain her fucked-up move. "I mean...I may have embellished a teensy-weensy bit. But I don't see the harm when we're almost as good as engaged."

I felt Simon's arm slide around his mom's back, and I knew he was offering her comfort in case Tinsley was telling the truth. I need to end this quickly so neither of them suffered needlessly. "How in the fuck could we be almost engaged when I've never so much as taken you on a date? I haven't even seen you in more than half a year, and that was only because my mother invited you to her home for dinner."

Her hand went to her chest, and she took a step back. "Oh. Um, your parents said you were dragging your heels because of your grief over losing your brother. I was giving you the space they told me you needed."

My anger turned to fury upon hearing my parents had used Weston's death as part of whatever game they were playing. "I'm a grown-ass man, Tinsley. My parents have no say in who I date, let alone marry. If I wanted you for my wife, you'd damn well know it."

"But your company and my father's—"

"Stop." I held up my hand. "I don't have a company, and I sure as hell don't care enough about your father's business to enter into a loveless marriage. Go home. There's nothing for you here."

She paled, her eyes filling with tears before she whirled around to run in the opposite direction. I felt no guilt for ripping into her after the pain she'd caused Skylar and Simon.

"Talk about wild." Skylar shook her head. "I had no idea things like that happened in real life. I feel like we're on the set of a soap opera right now."

Simon's brows were drawn together. "She was some crazy lady?"

"Not crazy, just so used to getting whatever she wanted, it never crossed her mind that I wouldn't marry her."

Simon's bottom lip trembled as his gaze flicked between his mom and me. "I didn't know. I'm—"

Letting go of Skylar, I pulled him against his chest, cutting off the apology he was about to give me. "You never have to say you're sorry for looking out for your mom. She's lucky to have you."

Simon's head tipped back. "Yeah, but she's lucky to have you too, and I almost messed that up."

"What happened today is not your fault. This is all on my parents."

"I guess it's safe to say they aren't going to be too happy to hear about us?" Skylar jerked her chin in the direction Tinsley had just gone. "If that's the kind of woman your parents were hoping you'd end up with, there's no way in heck they're going to approve of me."

"I stopped giving a damn about getting my parents' stamp of approval on what I'm doing a long time ago. Their priorities are messed up. If losing Weston wasn't enough to make them take a hard look at what's truly important, I have a feeling nothing is ever going to change that." I wrapped my fingers around her wrist and pulled her against my chest, my other hand sliding down her back before coming to a stop just above the curve of her ass. "If they don't accept your place in my life, that's their problem. Not ours."

She tilted her head farther back as she stared up at me. "And what exactly is my place, Baxter?"

"By my side for the rest of our lives." Lowering both my arms, I slid a hand into my pocket to retrieve the ring box I'd grabbed from my glove compartment earlier. Then I dropped to one knee and flipped the lid open with my thumb. "Skylar Hicks, I love you more than I ever thought possible, and the feeling somehow continues to grow every day. I never want there to be a time when you're not in my life, by my side, making everything better just by being you. Will you do me the honor of becoming my wife?"

She pressed trembling fingers against her lips as tears welled in her beautiful blue eyes. "Are you really saying you love me for the first time and proposing all at once? After we confronted the delusional woman who thought she'd marry you just because your parents told her she would?"

"Sorry, beautiful. I didn't think you were ready to hear it before, and I couldn't properly explain your place in my life without proposing." I pulled the white gold ring set with a pear-shaped, blue diamond out of the box and slipped it onto the tip of her finger. "Do you love me?"

She nodded, one of the tears spilling down her cheek. "Yes, I love you."

Hearing those three little words from her sweet lips meant everything. I hadn't planned to propose to Skylar anytime soon, but Tinsley's antics had pushed my timetable up. It was almost as though she'd pressed fast-forward, hurtling us through our first major stumbling block. And we'd come through it together, better than we'd been before. For the first time since I'd found out about the stunt Tinsley pulled, I didn't want to strangle the spoiled socialite. Not that I'd ever forgive her for hurting Skylar and Simon.

"Do you want to marry me?"

"So very much."

"She definitely does."

Mother and son spoke in unison, making me laugh as I slid the ring onto Skylar's finger.

Skylar sighed as she stared down at her hand. "It's so beautiful."

When the jeweler showed me this ring, I knew right away that it was the perfect choice for Skylar.

The three-carat stone wasn't so big that she'd feel uncomfortable wearing it—unless she ever found out what I'd paid for it, then she'd probably want to lock the ring in a vault—and the design was classically romantic. "Beautiful enough for you to accept it?"

"Yes, but it's going to be a long engagement. We need some time to become a family before I walk down the aisle to you."

"Whenever you want, beautiful. Just so long as I know it's going to happen, I can wait." As impatient as I was to officially make her mine, I knew she was right. "Weston would have loved you for me."

"And my parents are going to love you." I really hoped she was right because the last thing we needed was additional parent drama. Mine were going to bring more than enough with them.

# 22

The house was silent as I dragged Baxter away from my son's room. After all of the drama we'd gone through today, I was relieved that he'd been able to fall asleep so easily. But it had seemed as though the weight he'd been carrying the past week had finally lifted off his shoulders now that we'd discussed what he'd learned about his dad. After the showdown with that Tinsley woman—and Baxter's proposal—we'd returned to my house. The guys had bonded over a video game and my chocolate sheet cake while I made dinner. Baxter had loved the bacon-wrapped pork tenderloin so much that I decided to make it for his birthday every year. Another happy tradition for the little family we were building.

Simon's snores followed us into the hall, where we both tiptoed to my room like two high schoolers trying to sneak out. The whole thing would be laughable if that small alarm wasn't going off in my head that we might wake Simon up.

Whenever we were at Baxter's house, I didn't have to worry about keeping quiet, but here? Shaking my head, I forced those thoughts out of my brain. Since we were officially together now, there would be more times like this. Simon really liked Baxter and had given our engagement his blessing, and that meant more time with him staying over.

We sneaked inside my room and shut the door, putting as many barriers between us and the other parts of the house as we could. Baxter looked down at me, his eyes shining with love as we both giggled. Well, honestly, I giggled. In all the times I'd heard him laugh, giggling was definitely not the word to describe his deep chuckle.

"I finally have you all to myself. Just what I wanted for my birthday." He slid his hands up my front and cupped my breasts, rubbing my nipples with his thumbs. They pebbled at his touch, begging for more attention. With a wide grin, he pinched them, drawing out a soft moan. Leaning up, I puckered my lips, demanding a kiss, but he didn't oblige.

Instead, Baxter bent down and tossed me over his shoulder like he did that first night.

Shoving a fist in my mouth, I stifled the scream that hovered in my throat as he carried me to the bed. The last thing I needed was my teenage son bursting in and seeing his mother being hauled around like this. With playful swats, I pummeled his back, keeping my touch light so as not to cause yet another loud type of sound.

He plopped me onto the bed and stared down at me, his lips pulling up into a wolfish grin. "I know you're afraid of making too much noise," he murmured, unbuttoning his shirt. "But you can always scream into one of these pillows if you need to." Baxter winked as he slid his hand into his pocket before dropping his pants, revealing the hard length of his cock.

My mouth watered as I stared at him bobbing in front of me before drifting to his hands where he worked at the condom wrapper. It was sweet that he was always prepared to protect me, but we didn't need it. Not now. Not after everything.

I stood and placed my hands on his, bringing them up to kiss his knuckles. "I'm fine with going bare. Besides, I'm on birth control. It's fine."

His eyes crinkled as he smiled down at me. "I

didn't want to assume. I know we'd had conversations, but I never want you to think that I would ever take something this important for granted."

Tears pricked my eyes at his consideration. Dropping my hand, I wrapped my fingers around his girth, sighing at the soft groan vibrating through him. "I want to feel you tonight. All of you. Make love to me, Bax," I whispered against his flushed skin.

"I've never gone bare before." He dropped the condom to the floor and eased me back onto the bed. With adept movements, my clothes were quickly disposed of to follow his to the floor. "Hard and fast or soft and slow, no matter how I take you, it's always with love."

"I know. I can feel it." Sighing, I lay back as he spread my thighs and licked his lips. I never knew a man could love oral so much. I'd read about that in romance novels but never thought it could be real.

Instead of just going down on me, Baxter stared, a slow smile curving his lips. His tongue slid out again as if he savored the thought of me. Slowly, he leaned in his cheek grazing my inner thigh. His thumbs spread me open as he dragged the tip of his tongue across my clit. The touch was electric, lighting me up from the inside out.

Grabbing a nearby pillow, I brought the edge

over to my mouth. There was no way I'd be able to hold out without making any sounds. Whimpers clawed at the back of my throat as he lavished his attentions on me. Over and over, he drew small circles with his tongue, edging me ever closer to my release.

My body coiled as he continued to lick, and for a moment, I thought I would come on his tongue alone. As I reached the point of no return, he pulled back, leaving me bereft. Groaning, I chucked the pillow at him, laughing softly when he ducked. It sailed over his shoulder and landed on the floor with a light plop.

His breath tickled my skin as he leaned back in and started the process again. He started and stopped at least four times that I could remember, and my arousal built until it almost hurt. I needed to get off so desperately. But again, he pulled back away as I neared the peak number five.

"Please," I whimpered, struggling to keep my voice down. "I-I really need—"

My words were cut off as Baxter rose to his knees and pulled my hips close to his. The tip of his cock slid against my lower lips and bumped my clit, dragging another tortured moan from my lips. It was so different with him not wearing a condom. He was so warm against my skin. Without that barrier, I could feel all of him.

"Don't worry, beautiful," he whispered. "I'm going to take good care of you."

Pulling back, he surged deep inside, filling me with one stroke. My fingers fluttered over the covers as my hands sought out another pillow. Baxter leaned over, the devilish smirk never leaving his face, and grabbed one that was just out of reach. I snatched it from him and held it over my face, groaning as he pulled his cock out of me, only to slam back home.

There was none of his usual dirty talk, but I didn't need it. I was already close to the edge, and I felt his love for me in each movement of his body.

His fingers felt like fire as they dug into me, keeping me still so he could fuck me with wild abandon. The tendrils of an orgasm tightened through my body as his shaft slid against me, drawing out my pleasure. When his fingers went to my clit again, I was lost. White colored my vision as the orgasm I had been denied slammed into me, the sensations coalescing into the hardest release of my life.

I kept the pillow firmly in place as he continued to pump in and out. Each time he surged in and dragged out, my core fluttered about again as if I were having smaller orgasms each time. It was unreal. His hands snatched the pillow away from me for a moment, and he bit down into it, silencing his own roar of completion.

Baxter remained motionless for several moments, his cock pulsing deep inside. It felt so good. Perfect.

Then he dropped the pillow onto the bed and leaned down, sliding his lips over mine. "I don't want to leave you, but we need to get cleaned up. Especially since I wasn't wearing a condom."

That thought hadn't actually formulated in my brain. Of course, it would be a lot messier. Twisting to the side, I grabbed a handful of tissues and handed them to him, smiling as he brought them between our bodies. Luckily for us, my room came with an en suite bathroom, so his shuffle of shame wasn't all that far.

As with all the other times, he brought in a damp washcloth and made sure I was clean. Only this time, he returned it to my bathroom before sliding in behind to hold me close. His nose nuzzled my hair as he held me tightly against him, as though he never wanted to let me go. Truth be told, that feeling went both ways. I would never give him up. Ever.

My thoughts became fuzzy as I started to drift off

to sleep, but even in the sensual haze, I still heard him whispering how much he loved me.

With all the strength I could muster, I turned over to face him, my lips curling into a soft grin. "I love you so much," I whispered back, kissing him before laying my head on his chest. Whatever he said after, "I love you too," was swallowed up by the steady beating of his heart as it lulled me to sleep.

I felt safe in his arms, intertwined with his body. The heat between us was cozy and warm, helping me drift off. This was certainly the stuff of dreams, and I planned to soak up every minute of our time together. Though I didn't know what would happen tomorrow, next week, next year, or even in the next decade, I knew I didn't have to face any of it alone ever again.

W aking up with Skylar in my arms and my ring on her finger was the perfect start to my day. Unfortunately, the rest of it wasn't going to go quite as well since we would be having a showdown with my parents in front of the rest of my family. Not wanting to ruin our day together after all the drama yesterday, I'd put off talking to her about dinner for as long as I could. But now that we needed to head over there in less than an hour, I couldn't wait any longer.

"I know this is a big ask with very little notice, but with everything that happened yesterday, I've been putting off talking to you about the surprise dinner my grandparents are throwing for me. Will you come?"

Skylar's eyes widened. "You want me to come to a Moore family dinner?'

"Not just you. I want Simon to come too." Even though tonight was going to suck, I wanted her son to start to get to know my family better. Except for my parents, who had a lot of work they needed to do if they wanted to be a part of our lives. "If things go my way, your family is going to grow by a fuck of a lot. I have plenty of cousins I'm more than willing to share and lots of aunts and uncles who'll be thrilled to spoil Simon since they don't have any grandchildren yet."

"Aw, yes. We'd love to join you. When is it?"

This was the tricky part. "Tonight."

"Wait," she gasped, her hand going to her chest, my diamond sparkling on her finger. "The dinner that woman mentioned is real? It's happening tonight at your grandparents' house?"

I nodded. "Yup."

"And your parents are going to be there?"

Another nod. "Unfortunately, yes."

"Then we will absolutely be there. How much time do I have to get ready?" I didn't know what caused the fire that lit her eyes, but I was glad that her ire didn't seem to be aimed at me for giving her so little time to prepare.

"Thirty minutes."

"I can work with that." She dropped a quick kiss on my lips before scrambling off the couch to yell, "Simon, get cleaned up and put on some nice clothes. We're going to Franklin and Katherine Moore's house for dinner to celebrate Baxter's birthday."

He came running up the stairs from the basement, his gaze searching me out when he realized his mom had already disappeared into her room. "That dinner is really happening? With your parents?" he unknowingly echoed his mom's earlier question.

I nodded. "It is."

"Damn." He rubbed his hands together. "This is more drama than the television shows the girls at school like to watch."

I laughed as he headed upstairs to get changed. Now that he'd cleared the air with Skylar about his dad and didn't think I was cheating on her, Simon was back to being a typical teenager. Which apparently included not minding family drama as long as his mom was happy. If only I could be as laid-back as him.

By the time we pulled into my grandparents' driveway, tension was coiled tight in my body. Skylar reached over and smoothed her hand down my arm. "We can go out to dinner somewhere else if you don't want to be here. I'm sure your grandparents would understand."

"I know they would, but I want to get this crap with my parents over and done with while they're in town," I muttered as I shut off the truck's engine. "If they follow the same pattern, we won't have to worry about seeing them again for another forty or so years unless we decide to visit them."

I sounded as bitter as I felt, and Simon ducked his head between the seats to pat me on the shoulder. "Don't worry. Mom and I have your back."

I dropped my head and took a slow breath, deeply touched that this sixteen-year-old boy understood the meaning of family better than my parents. "Thanks, Simon. That means a lot to me."

"Ready?" Skylar asked.

"Yup, let's do this."

When I circled the truck to open Skylar's door, Simon grinned at me. The approving gleam in his eyes was a far cry from the pain that had been there yesterday, and I was damn happy he'd bounced back so quickly.

We presented a united front as we walked up the steps to the house. Rigden opened the door before we got there, with Dean at his back. My cousins normally would have smiled in greeting, but there wasn't even a gleam of good humor in their expressions. My parents had definitely arrived before us.

"Don't worry, guys. It'll all be okay." I lifted Skylar's hand so they could see my ring on her finger. "They can either get on board with my plans and beg for forgiveness"—they knew my parents well enough to snort over that possibility—"or lose the chance to be a part of our lives."

"Congratulations."

"Happy for you, man."

My cousins kept their voices low and clapped me on the back as we walked past. They must have warned everyone else about the confrontation I was going to have with my parents tonight. My aunts, uncles, cousins, and grandparents were on one side of the room with my mom and dad on the other, and none of them joined in when my parents yelled, "Surprise!"

"Mom, Dad. What are you doing here?"

My dad was not happy with my lukewarm greeting. He went straight into defensive mode. "In Mooreville? I grew up here, and now you live here. Why wouldn't I be here?"

His response was ridiculous considering how long it had been since he'd visited his parents. "Excellent question, Dad. One you probably should have considered years ago over any of the holidays or birthdays we missed out on spending with the family. This situation isn't the slightest bit funny, but it's ironic as fuck."

"Language, Baxter," my mother chided

"I'm almost forty, well past the point when I need to follow your rules, or you need to interfere in my life."

My mom sighed and shook her head. "It doesn't matter how old you are. You'll always be our son."

That was the same bullshit they'd trotted out when they'd been trying to convince my brother to give up on his dream of being a fireman to do what they wanted instead. "I'm not really feeling the love right now. Not when I'm just being honest. If you being so damn fired up for grandchildren that you keep throwing women at me but then almost fucking up your only chance of getting them isn't ironic, I don't know what is."

My mom's brows drew together. "What?"

I felt Simon at my back, just where he'd said he would be. Jerking my thumb over my shoulder, I explained, "Tinsley flew her ass out here and ran her mouth to my woman's son. Told him she's my fiancé. Made him think I was cheating on his mom. Your games gutted a sixteen-year-old boy who deserves a fuck of a lot better from the people who're going to become his grandparents when I marry his mother."

My mom pressed her hand to her chest. "Oh, dear. We invited Tinsley to come with us to Mooreville as our guest, but I didn't realize you'd bumped into her. She wasn't at the hotel when we arrived this afternoon."

My deep chuckle held no humor. "That's all you got out of what I just said?"

"There's no need to take that tone with your mother. She meant well. It's not her fault if Tinsley said some things that weren't exactly true."

My dad's lame attempt at ducking responsibility only pissed me off more. "There wasn't even a smidgen of truth in what she said, which you would damn well know if you didn't have your head so far up your ass that you can't see what's right in front of your face."

"You can't talk to me like that," he roared, his face turning red.

"You're still not listening to me. Mom, Dad, meet Skylar. She's your future daughter-in-law. Not Tinsley." I lifted Skylar's hand and pressed a kiss against the soft skin directly above where my ring rested on her finger. "Fuck things up with her even more, and you will have lost any chance of building a relationship with my wife, Simon, and any other children we might have."

"You can't just kick us out of your lives," my dad blustered.

My mom crossed her arms over her chest with a huff. "Not unless you want to lose your family trust."

I laughed so hard at her threat, I had to bend over to catch my breath before I could speak. "You want to yank my inheritance? Go ahead. I'll write you a check for the ten million I already got from your parents if that's what it takes to get you to understand how serious I am about this."

"Baxter, no," Skylar whispered, her hand trembling on my arm.

I wrapped my arm around her back. "Don't worry, beautiful. What my parents fail to understand is that I don't need their money. I have more than enough of my own. It'll take me less than half a year to make that up on interest alone."

"It isn't the money. I don't care about that." My parents looked shocked at her words, but I knew how true they were. "I just don't want you to say something you might regret later."

My grandfather moved close, his lips curled into a deep frown, looking older than his years. "I think we're well past saying something we'll regret later, but it's my son who should be ashamed. Not my grandson. Baxter is just standing up for the sweet, beautiful woman he's chosen to spend the rest of his life with. As he should."

"We don't even know a thing about her," my dad argued.

"You might not, but the rest of the family knows her quite well. Baxter and Skylar have more than our approval. They have our blessing and well wishes for a happy marriage." My grandfather shook his head. "Unfortunately, you've missed out on the opportunity to see how perfectly matched they are. And seeing as I'm going to have to ask you to leave, you won't be getting it any time soon."

No matter how much my dad argued, my grandfather wouldn't budge, and they finally left. I wasn't sure if my parents and I were ever going to repair our relationship. But with the rest of the Moores offering their congratulations on our engagement, I knew my parents were the ones missing out. Family was everything.

## EPILOGUE
SKYLAR

My long engagement ended up only being six months, which was about five more than Baxter had hoped for. After the argument with his parents, things settled down and we were able to figure out how the three of us fit together as a family. And when Simon got to see firsthand how big Baxter's house was—and how awesome it was to have a chef available to cook for you—he'd teamed up with Baxter to convince me that it wasn't too early for us to move in. It had only taken them a month to wear me down, and Dean found a buyer for my old house six weeks after that. Adding in the opening of Leaves & Pages, I had a lot going on at once. But it was all incredible, and I had so much support.

With the help of his grandmother, aunts, my

mom, and Sarah, I was able to throw together an incredible wedding in less than two months...precipitated by the positive pregnancy test that had shocked both of us. We'd talked about having another child, but with my age, I thought it would take a while to happen. It turned out that I hadn't even had the chance to come off birth control before my sexy fiancé managed to knock me up.

I'd been happily married for the past five months and over the morning sickness that had alerted us to my pregnancy for most of that time. And my two favorite men had been conspiring against me since before the wedding, ever since we found out I was pregnant. I could barely lift a finger without one of them hovering. Like right now, as I tried to take a customer's order.

"Sit down. I'll make her tea," Baxter insisted after the woman told me what she wanted.

"And I'll grab some more scones from the back to restock the display case," Simon offered.

"Do they make them all like him here?" the customer asked as she held a ten-dollar bill out.

I shook my head. "Sorry, Baxter didn't grow up in Mooreville."

"Darn." She snapped her fingers. "There went my chance to find the perfect man."

I flashed her a quick grin. "Well, he does have lots of male cousins who are an awful lot like him."

"Really?" she purred, with a speculative gleam in her eyes. "I guess I'll have to become one of your regulars so you can let me know when one of them visits. I don't have time to peruse the books today, so it'll give me the perfect excuse to look them all over. Or are the books my excuse to look your husband's cousins over? I think I might've gotten my story mixed up."

I laughed at the thought of her staking out my shop in the hope of catching a glimpse of one of Baxter's many cousins. "Oh, did I forget to mention they all live here?"

"Dang, girl. Way to bury the lede." She laughed as she picked up her to-go cup after Baxter set it down on the counter. "Too bad I'm not really in a position to start a relationship. But you can count on me to come in and enjoy the eye candy once I get settled into my new place."

"Sounds like a great plan to me. You can try our different tea blends and baked goods while you look them over. The books, I mean. Or Baxter's cousins, whichever will make you a regular since I can use as many of those as I can get."

"With as cute as this place is"—she opened the

pastry bag Baxter set in front of her and took a big whiff—"and as amazing as the baked goods smell, you can count on me being here a lot."

Squinting at the woman as I held out her change, I couldn't shake the feeling that I knew her from somewhere. "Are you new to Mooreville? Because you seem so familiar to me."

"Yeah, I get that a lot." She lifted one shoulder. "I think it's because of my brown hair and eyes. Makes me seem like I could be anyone, really."

I didn't see how that was possible since she was drop-dead gorgeous, but she didn't give me the chance to ask anything else before she swiveled on her heel and walked toward the door.

Baxter wrapped his arms around me from behind and rested his chin on my shoulder. "Hmm, maybe I'll get the chance to play wingman for one of my cousins. That could be fun."

"With who?" Simon asked as he returned, holding a tray piled high with scones.

Baxter lifted his chin toward the customer who was leaving with her tea and muffin. "I should start with her since she's the one who gave me the idea."

"The lady who just bought a cup of Earl Gray and a blueberry muffin?" Simon asked, shaking his head. "I don't think so."

My brows drew together. "How come?"

He shrugged before crouching down to open the back of the display case. "I can't imagine she'll stick around Mooreville for long."

Simon sounded as though there was a reason he thought she'd leave town soon. "Wait, do you know who she is?"

He tilted his head back and lifted a single brow. "Uh, yeah."

"From where? I feel like I know her, but I can't quite place how."

Simon stood and handed the tray of scones to Baxter. Then he pulled his phone out of his back pocket and tapped at the screen. "Huh, that's weird. Her account isn't here anymore."

"What account? Where?" I asked, placing my hands on my hips.

"She's a huge influencer on social media, but it looks like she took her account down." He let out a low whistle. "She had like twenty million followers and was making bank. Something had to have made her walk away from that kind of easy money."

"I wonder what," I murmured as the woman climbed into a Porsche Taycan parked in front of the store.

Baxter set the tray down on the counter and

palmed my rounded belly. "You can wonder all you want, but if she's wrapped up in some drama, you're going to stay very, very far away from it. Stress isn't good for you right now."

"Fine," I huffed. Our baby was going to be here soon enough. If the mysterious influencer was still around, I could meddle all I wanted then. It would be easy enough to make sure Dean popped in sometime if she was here perusing the books. I owed him for being Baxter's wingman, after all. And he could do a whole lot worse than a gorgeous, confident, and successful woman.

Curious about what might happen between the mysterious influencer and Dean? You'll find out in Can't Take Moore!

Have you grabbed Sucked Into Love for FREE yet?

# THE COMING HOME SERIES

The Coming Home Series ... Let love guide you home.

Each story in this series is crafted around the same premise—what does it mean to come home? Twelve standalone stories, one per month from a different author, will fill you with heat and heart.

Welcome home.

Click here for The Coming Home Series page

Join our Facebook neighborhood

## ABOUT THE AUTHOR

I absolutely adore reading—always have and always will. When I was growing up, my friends used to tease me when I would trail after them, trying to read and walk at the same time. If I have downtime, odds are you will find me reading or writing.

I am the mother of two wonderful sons who have inspired me to chase my dream of being an author. I want them to learn from me that you can live your dream as long as you are willing to work for it.

*Connect with me online:*

Printed in Great Britain
by Amazon

85492716R00153